LACK OF
EVIDENCE

OTHER BOOKS AND BOOKS ON CASSETTE
BY DAN YATES:

Eyes of an Angel

Angels Don't Knock

Just Call Me an Angel

Angels to the Rescue

An Angel in the Family

It Takes an Angel

An Angel's Christmas

Angel on Vacation

An Angel in Time

LACK OF EVIDENCE

A NOVEL

DAN YATES

Covenant Communications, Inc.

Cover image © EyeWire/GettyImages

Cover design copyrighted 2003 by Covenant Communications, Inc.

Published by Covenant Communications, Inc.
American Fork, Utah

Printed in the United States of America
First Printing: May 2003

10 09 08 07 06 05 04 03   10 9 8 7 6 5 4 3 2 1

ISBN 1-59156-206-6

Library of Congress Cataloging-in-Publication Data

Yates, Dan, 1934-
    Lack of evidence: a novel / Dan Yates.
        p.   cm.
    ISBN 1-59156-206-6
    1. Inheritance and succession--Fiction. 2. Fathers and sons--Fiction. 3. Missing persons--Fiction. 4. Mormons-- Fiction. I. Title.

PS3575.A763L33 2003
813'.54--dc21

                                                        2003043440

DEDICATION

When I was born, you were there to hold me. When I was a child, you were there to guide and protect me. When I was married, you were there to cheer me on. As my children and grandchildren were born, you were there to love them. Now, it's time for you to go. I can't imagine what life will be like without you only a phone call away, big sister. But I know when the time comes for me to go home, you'll be there to meet me at the door. And we'll never say good-bye again. I love you, Pauline, and I dedicate the words of this story to you.

PROLOGUE

Attending funerals wasn't one of Reggie's favorite things to do. Most were depressing, and the overpowering smell of flowers often left her nauseous. But this funeral was different. Not because she was the one chosen to give the eulogy, but because the man being paid homage this morning was one of the greatest Reggie had ever met. She had known this man long before the day when Derrick returned home from his years in Oahu, but it was after Derrick's return that he became so very special to her. Glancing down at the closed mahogany casket in front of the podium, she brushed away a tear and almost wished she weren't the one delivering the eulogy. She wasn't sure if she could find words strong enough.

Reggie caught her breath as the bishop stood and moved to the pulpit. After a long pause to gather his courage, the bishop spoke. "We'd like to welcome everyone here this morning. From my point of view, I can verify the wisdom in holding these services at the stake center. I can't spot so much as one empty seat. A fitting testimonial to the man I've called *Father* all my life."

Tears welled up in Reggie's eyes, and her heart felt as if it would explode. The love she felt for this bishop was also something words could never adequately express. It hadn't always been that way. She often wondered how things might have turned out if Derrick had chosen to remain on the islands instead of returning home when he did. But, happily, this was a question that would never need be asked.

CHAPTER 1

Derrick Beatty paid the fare, then watched as the cab pulled away down the one-lane country road, leaving a cloud of dust rolling in its wake. Picking up his suitcases, Derrick turned to look at the old house. Not much had changed in the four years since he last saw it. If the condition of the outside was any indication, the neighbor he had engaged to look after things had given him his money's worth. Derrick filled his lungs with fresh autumn air that smelled like no other place but home could smell. While four and a half years living in the tropical setting of Oahu was nothing to complain about, Oahu just wasn't home. When the phone call came from Clint Banister offering Derrick his old job back at the detective agency, it had caught Derrick by complete surprise. Until then, he'd given no thought to ever living stateside again.

Derrick moved the length of the sidewalk, stopping for only a moment when he reached the wooden steps leading up to the porch. Slowly, he placed his weight on the first step to hear the familiar old creak that had been there for as long as he could remember. This brought a smile and a flood of memories. He always wondered why his dad never fixed that old step. Right now, he was glad he hadn't, as the sound of it had a way of making the old house seem more like home. Maybe his dad understood and that's why he never bothered to fix it.

Derrick set the suitcases on the porch and dug a ring of keys from his pocket. The house key was still attached. He could never bring himself to remove it, even while living thousands of miles and half an ocean away. A lot of people thought he should have put the house up for sale when he moved away, but he didn't have the heart to do that either. This house was almost as much a part of him as was his own name. He unlocked the door and shoved it open, looking at the dim interior, where more memories leapt out to greet him. Moving the suitcases inside, he set them down, closed the door, then painstakingly made his way through the hall to the kitchen. Here he visualized his mother in her crisp white apron and could almost smell the bread baking in the oven. He grinned to himself, thinking how he'd give a thousand dollars for a single slice of his mother's special potato bread about now. He'd never tasted bread like it since the day she had died.

Moving to the den, Derrick envisioned his father at work on one of his paintings. Derrick was always intrigued at how his father could take a simple sheet of canvas and bring it to life with an Arizona sunset, children playing in a garden, or whatever else he felt inspired to paint. Samuel Beatty was an industrious man who believed in the principle of work. But when there was a rare minute for himself, Samuel would spend it in one of two ways—painting in the den or boring holes through cotton candy clouds in his shiny yellow, open-cockpit biplane. Samuel's love for flying had most certainly rubbed off on his son Derrick, even if his talent for painting had not.

Over the years, Samuel had created hundreds of paintings, but only three remained in the house now. Samuel was well-known for giving his art to friends or family who expressed a liking for a particular piece, but the charity stopped when it came to these three paintings. One had hung over the fireplace since long before Derrick and his brother were born. It was a painting of Samuel and Evelana against a scene of the Arizona temple, where they were sealed for time and all eternity.

The second of the three paintings hung on the living room wall, where it could be seen by anyone entering the house. This one depicted Evelana in a high-back wicker chair with her two fifteen-year-old sons standing on each side of her. Derrick and Corbin were twins, with Derrick being the older by three and a half minutes. The fact that they weren't identical went far beyond physical looks. Evelana often compared Derrick to a mountain—firm and enduring, a man who knew exactly what he wanted and where to find it. Corbin she thought of as a rainbow, with flashes of glory that all too soon vanished into the darkness of a storm.

The last of the three paintings hung over the desk in Samuel's old office. This was a painting of Samuel and his partner, Herb Solomon, standing in front of their gold mine in the rugged Arizona mountains. Sadly enough, though the mine had brought wealth to both men, neither had ever enjoyed the fruits of their fortune.

Glancing through the window on the far wall of the den, Derrick could see the old backyard where he and Corbin played every boy's game from cops and robbers to hide-and-seek to kick-the-can. The two of them had been inseparable as boys, and their trouble didn't start until years later. Thinking about this brought an ache to Derrick's heart. He missed the days when he and Corbin had been so close. Miss them or not, they were days gone forever. Hard as it was to admit, the best thing Derrick thought he and Corbin could do at this stage of their lives was to keep as much distance between them as possible.

Derrick stepped back to the living room, where he retrieved the suitcases. As he did, the painting of himself with Corbin and their mother caught his eye. Whatever happened to the boy he was back then? The boy had obviously faded into oblivion and reemerged as a man searching for answers to so many of life's questions. Strange how the years had only deepened the questions instead of supplying the answers.

Taking the suitcases, Derrick moved to the bedroom, where he set to work unpacking them. It took only a short time to put away the few things he had personally brought from the islands. Most of what he owned wouldn't arrive for days since it was being shipped. He could make do with what he had. Of course, he'd need to do some shopping for groceries, toiletries, household products, that sort of thing. But it wouldn't take much to set up housekeeping again. Being a bachelor made it easier.

With the unpacking finished, he moved back to the kitchen, where he spotted a note from Fred Lockhart lying on the counter. Fred lived in a house just down the road and was the man Derrick had engaged to care for things while he was away. The note read, *Welcome back, old friend. I think you'll find everything in order. Your baby's in the garage, just waiting for you. I had it detailed and serviced as soon as I learned you were on your way home. Barbara says to tell you she'll cook you up a real proper homecoming meal when you get settled in. She would like a day's warning. Give us a call.*

The note brought a smile. Derrick would take Barbara up on her offer—she was one heck of a cook. Marrying Barbara was probably the smartest thing Fred had ever done. Picking up the set of keys lying next to the note, Derrick made a beeline for the garage. Flipping on the light brought a thrill as he spotted the car sitting there, just where he had left it four and a half years earlier. It was a brilliant red 1962 Corvette convertible. Samuel had bought the car and had it restored while Derrick was still in high school with the understanding that it would become Derrick's on the day he returned home from his mission. Samuel had purchased a second car, too—a jet-black 1960 Ford Thunderbird, which was slated for Corbin at the end of his mission. The Thunderbird had been placed in storage, where it remained to that very day.

The Corvette had always been Derrick's pride and joy. Leaving it behind when he moved to Oahu wasn't easy, but the expense of having it shipped overseas was a little too steep, so it had remained. He opened the door and slid behind the wheel. It felt like finding an old friend after years in different worlds.

When Derrick had taken the call from Clint and realized it was to offer his old job back, his first inclination was to flatly decline, yet Clint wouldn't hear of it. "Oh, no you don't, Mr. Beatty!" he argued. "You're not turning me down without even taking time to consider my offer! Say yes and I'll double your old salary."

"Double my salary?" Derrick gasped. "You really do want me back, don't you?"

"Hey, I've tried filling your shoes four times since you've been gone. Not one replacement worked out. I need you desperately. And if you'll be honest with yourself, you'll realize you need to come home!"

"Clint, I . . ."

"Don't 'Clint I' me. I'm hanging up now, but I'll call you back in a week. I'll accept your answer then, provided it's a yes. Otherwise, we'll talk some more."

At first Derrick told himself there was nothing to consider. But after the first two sleepless nights, he had to admit that wasn't quite true. Considering the offer made no sense, though. Except for his burning desire to reopen the case of his father's disappearance, Derrick didn't think there was really a good reason for him to entertain thoughts of going home. It would be bad enough returning to the emptiness left by his parents both being gone even if he didn't have to face Reggie again. Not one day had gone by when Derrick didn't think about Reggie. More nights than he cared to remember, he had dreamed of her deep green eyes and soft black hair. Derrick and Reggie had worked as partners before he quit the agency and moved to Oahu. He had no idea when he had fallen in love with her—all he knew was that he'd never found the heart to tell her. Yet maybe it wasn't the fact he *hadn't* found the heart to tell her. Maybe the truth was stronger than that. Maybe it was more like he *couldn't* find the heart to tell her. Reggie wasn't the first woman Derrick had fallen in love with. His first love had come when he was a very young man. Her name was Vivian Lane, and before the final curtain fell between them, there was much more involved than just Derrick's broken heart. It was a life-shattering experience with scars much too deep to be soon forgotten, and it left Derrick terrified of giving his heart again.

When Walden Stewart first entered the picture as potential competition for Reggie's attention, Derrick told himself it would likely last about as long as any of the other of Reggie's here-today-and-gone-tomorrow romances. And even if it didn't, so what? Reggie was her own woman. If she chose to date Walden or anyone else, what business was it of Derrick's? But Walden did something Derrick wasn't expecting. He proposed. And Reggie had said yes.

That's when Derrick had done one of the dumbest things of his life. What could he have been thinking? If he was going to propose to someone just to get back at Reggie, why, of all people, had he chosen Brandilynne McDowell? He should have known a woman with the social status of Brandilynne would find a way to splash the news all over the city. She had really outdone herself on that one. The announcement party she had thrown included a guest list of everyone from the mayor to the managing editor of the *Arizona Republic*. By the time Derrick came to his senses and decided to call the engagement off, he discovered it wasn't going to be all that easy. Brandilynne was willing to let him off the hook, but only on her terms. He wasn't allowed to tell anyone about their breakup until she was ready to make the announcement herself. Though Brandilynne didn't come right out and say it, Derrick was positive she wanted to keep up appearances until after she met someone else to take his place. And so it was that for the first two years Derrick was on Oahu, the general public was led to believe he and Brandilynne were still a couple.

Derrick didn't care all that much about what the rest of the world thought, but he wished Reggie had known the truth. Not that he knew why, really. He just wished she knew. Derrick didn't think it would have changed things much, though. Reggie was in love with another man, one she would marry regardless of what Derrick might do. But he still wished she had known the truth. As much as he hated to admit it at the time, losing Reggie tore him apart. This, added to the pain of his father's disappearance, had been too much to handle. Then he had resigned from Banister's agency and moved halfway across an ocean.

There had never been one word from Reggie. Derrick sort of expected a wedding announcement, but one never came. He could only wonder why, yet he had neither the courage nor the inclination to ask. The only stateside people he communicated with were Fred and Barbara Lockhart, who didn't run in the same social circles as Derrick's old acquaintances. Fred and Barbara had their own friends.

True to his word, Clint did call back. By the time he did, Derrick had reached one of the most difficult decisions of his life. The thing that finally tipped the scales in Clint's favor was Derrick's burning desire to make a stab at learning what really happened to his father. "All right, Clint," Derrick consented. "I'm probably out of my mind for this, but I'll go to work for you again on one condition."

"Name it," Clint responded without the slightest hesitation. "If it's in my power, we'll talk turkey."

"I want to reopen my dad's case," Derrick explained. "I'll handle your other caseloads, naturally, but I want to do some research to see if I can learn the truth about Dad's disappearance."

"I got no problem at all with that, buddy. I know you'll give me my just due. No one would like to see the mystery of your dad solved more than I would. I'll put all the facilities of the agency behind your research, and I'll even promise not to over-load you for the first few weeks so you can spend most of your time on Samuel's case. So how about it? Do we have a deal?"

Derrick explained he'd need two weeks to get everything in

order, and another week to make the trip home. Clint agreed, and the die was cast. Why Derrick didn't ask about Reggie while he had Clint on the phone was still a question he had no answer for. In a way, he almost hoped she no longer worked for Clint. With a little luck, she might even have moved to another state. Derrick knew it would be so much easier if he didn't have to see her with Walden. Not that he didn't want her and Walden to be happy, he just didn't want to have to watch them being happy.

Derrick hit the button opening the automatic garage door. One twist of the key, and the Corvette roared to life. Tomorrow morning he'd have to face whatever was to be faced at his old job. For now, a ride through the country in the Corvette was in order. Somehow, he was sure coming home was the right decision. It felt great, and it was time he put some old ghosts to rest.

CHAPTER 2

Reggie Mandel couldn't believe her eyes as she pulled the Firebird into her regular parking spot outside the Banister Detective Agency. She did a double take and still couldn't believe what she was seeing.

"It's Derrick's Corvette," she muttered to herself. "I'd know that car anyplace. But why is it parked here in his old spot?"

Reggie hadn't seen the car since the day Derrick had quit his job and gone traipsing off to the Hawaiian Islands more than four years ago. She'd just assumed he had taken the car with him, since it was the thing he loved the most in the whole world. She killed the engine and stepped out of her car, figuring today was a good day to enter the office through the back door so as not to walk into any unwanted surprises.

Finding the back entrance unlocked, she pushed open the door and peered inside. From the angle she was at, she could barely see Derrick's old desk, but it was enough for her to see him seated at it. Jerking back, she closed the door and stood there, trying to catch her breath. After a moment, she cracked the door an inch and peered inside again to verify her imagination wasn't working overtime and that it really was Derrick. But what was he doing unpacking a cardboard box at his old desk?

"Oh!" she gasped as the reality suddenly struck her. "He's moving back in! How can this be?"

Reggie hadn't heard one word from Derrick in more than four years, and all at once here he was, moving back in. Her heart beat so frantically it was nearly a full minute before she could compose herself enough to ease through the door and make a mad dash for Clint's office. Thankfully, Derrick didn't seem to notice. She didn't bother to knock at Clint's office, but barged right in, hurriedly pulling the door closed behind her.

"What is Derrick Beatty doing here?" she whispered loud enough for Clint to hear but not loud enough for her voice to carry past the closed door. Clint's mouth curled up into a grin that Reggie had learned always preceded an unexpected bombshell. "Oh, no!" she gasped. "You've talked him into taking his old job back!"

Clint stood and rounded his desk. "I would have mentioned it sooner, but . . ."

"You'd have mentioned it sooner?" she shot back. "Well you know, that might have been nice! It would at least have given me the chance to prepare myself. I have half a mind to take a week off starting this very minute! You have a mile-wide cruel streak, you know that, Clint Banister!"

Clint held out a hand. "Now, now, now, Regg, take a deep breath and just relax. When the shock passes, you're going to thank me for hiring Derrick back. It's not like I'm blind to your real feelings for the guy."

Reggie hated Clint's ability to read her like a book. "I do not have feelings for him!" she fumed, knowing full well her lie was falling on deaf ears. "Derrick is an insensitive man who cares for nothing but his job, airplanes, and that stupid Corvette parked out there in the lot." She bit her lip and tried to force herself from saying the rest of what was pressing on her mind. She wanted to say something about Derrick probably being married by now, but somehow she managed to hold back. She knew that the Derrick and Brandilynne thing had never meshed. Brandilynne herself had made that plain when she and Albert

Hainsley had linked up. But it had been over four years, and Reggie knew Derrick might have met and married someone else. Clint's next statement made her wonder if he knew for sure that Derrick was still single or if he was just guessing.

"Not true, Regina. The guy's nuts about you. If you'd give him the slightest hint you might care for him too, he'd fall all over himself proving it."

Reggie shook her head in disgust and crossed the room to face Clint. "Let's get one thing straight," she staunchly insisted. "Derrick works with Earl. I'm perfectly happy with Chandra as my partner, and I don't want any ripples on the water."

Clint slid an arm around Reggie's shoulder and gave it a squeeze. "You know I always tag up a guy with a gal, Regg. Putting you with Chandra was temporary until I could fill the vacant spot."

"Fine! Then pair me up with Earl and put Derrick with Chandra!"

"Nope! You and Derrick were the best team I ever had working for me. I always say not to mess with perfection."

Reggie pulled back a step and glared at Clint, regretting that her hair had chosen today of all days to turn stubborn. And why had she worn these old Dockers and this ugly yellow top? "You had this planned all along, didn't you?" she fumed. "You figured some way to get Derrick back, and you knew from the first you'd put us back together!"

"Am I interrupting something? Should I come back later?"

The sound of Derrick's voice sent an icy chill running down her spine as Reggie whirled to see the door cracked open and his head peeking around it. How much of her conversation with Clint had he heard? One thing she knew for sure—the look on his face revealed he was obviously no more thrilled about this reunion than she was. "Nope, you're not interrupting a thing," she heard Clint respond. "Bring it in, pal, and let's get down to the nitty-gritty."

Reggie felt her heart pound as Derrick eased the door open and stepped into the room. For a long moment he paused, just looking at her. The years had been good to him, and if anything, he was better looking than ever. His hair was black, almost as black as her own, only his had a streak of silver over his left eye that had always intrigued her. His eyes were deep blue, and they had an almost hypnotic effect when he turned on his charm. Right now, it wasn't charm she saw in his eyes—it was something else. Anxiety? Concern? She wasn't quite sure. But it was obvious he was as ill at ease over this meeting as she was. Pulling back his shoulders, he walked over to face her. "Hi, Regg. You're looking good."

Reggie was a woman who didn't know the meaning of the word *fear.* She had looked down the business end of more than one loaded gun barrel and had confronted scoundrels of every sort and character. But at this moment, she wished she could turn and run as fast and as far as her legs would carry her. "Hi to you too," she heard herself say. "Or should that be *aloha?*"

He tried to laugh, but it sounded hollow. "I think I've had enough alohas for a while. It's sort of nice being on the mainland again."

"Okay," Clint broke in. "Enough of this chitchat. Let's cut to the chase. I've spoken to Regina about partnering the two of you up again, and she's pleased with the idea. How do you feel about the deal, Derrick?"

Reggie's mouth dropped as her eyes shot open. How could Clint say such a thing? He almost made it sound like pairing her and Derrick up had been *her* idea. She glanced to see that same indiscernible look still on Derrick's face. His answer came with apparent difficulty. "You're the boss, Clint. If the lady has no objection, then neither do I."

Clint put one arm around Reggie's shoulder and the other around Derrick. "Okay, then it's settled. Regina here isn't aware of the deal we worked out, Derrick, so I'll lay it out for her.

Derrick took his old job back on one condition, Regg. He wants the chance to do some checking on his dad's disappearance. I agreed and figured out a way to juggle our workload enough to give the two of you a couple of weeks' time to spend almost exclusively on Samuel's case."

This new revelation caught Reggie's interest. She personally had never spent any time on the mystery of Samuel's disappearance, but just about every other investigator in every capacity in these parts had scrutinized the case from the inside out. It wasn't that she didn't welcome the chance to add her talent to the search for the missing legend, but it was just that the effort seemed so futile. After all, every rock that could be turned had already been turned multiple times with no success. The mystery of Samuel's disappearance was no closer to being solved today than it was the day almost five years ago when he fell off the edge of the world.

It made perfect sense, though, that this was what brought Derrick home. Wanting to take one last shot at learning his father's fate was only natural. Reggie knew she would be lying to herself if she denied wishing she might have had some small part in his decision to come home, but she might as well face the truth that it was Samuel and Samuel alone who drew Derrick home.

"What about Melvin Phillips?" she asked Clint. "His court case comes up a week from tomorrow, and I have tons of work to do before completing the case the defense has asked for."

"Get me the file, Regina. I'll handle Melvin personally. His is a big-dollar case, and I want it done right."

There was no doubt in Reggie's mind that Clint had thought this all out way in advance. She fully realized the futility in arguing with the man once he had his mind made up. And whether or not she wanted to admit it to herself, Clint was right. In spite of her masquerade, she really was glad Derrick had come home—she just wasn't ready to show it yet. "All right," she agreed. "I'll turn Melvin over to you, Clint. But you'd better not blow it after all the time and energy I've put into proving the guy innocent."

"You don't know for sure he's innocent, Regg—not until we get the results back on the blood samples you sent to the lab. When are those results due, by the way?"

"They're due tomorrow, but don't tell me I'm not sure of my findings. The DNA won't match Melvin's. Take my word for it."

"Hey, I'm not doubting your word. If you tell me you're that sure, then so be it. And you can put your mind at ease. I won't drop the ball." Clint lowered his arms and turned to Derrick. "So, where do you want to start, pal? Got anything in mind?"

"I do if the agency's Cessna is available. I'd like to look over a couple of things."

Reggie grinned to herself at this request. Clint's detective agency may have been small, but since he refused to forgo the fun of owning his own plane, why shouldn't he list it as an agency resource? It made good sense when tax time rolled around. Derrick was the only other pilot who could use it. "The plane is yours," Clint responded. "As long as your license is up-to-date."

This brought a laugh. "Come on, Clint. Do you really believe I'd stay out of a cockpit for any length of time? What do you think I spent my Saturdays doing on Oahu?"

"I should have known." Clint grew strangely quiet, something out of the ordinary for him. When he spoke, it was with clear-cut difficulty. "Go ahead and get things squared away at your desk, Derrick. I'd like just a minute with Regina, if that's okay."

Reggie raised her brow, considering what this might be about. Derrick took the hint and headed for the door. If Clint's suggestion bothered him in the least, it didn't show. As the door closed, Reggie looked at Clint. "I want you to know what getting Derrick back means to me—to the agency, Regg. You know you've always been my number-one investigator. And you know you and Derrick made the number-one all-time team when he was here before."

"If you're trying to apologize to me for the way you handled this, don't bother, Clint. You couldn't have handled it worse if you'd called a staff meeting to brainstorm the ways. I'll work with Derrick, and I'm sure we'll get along just fine. Probably just about like we did before." Reggie laughed to herself. What more could she hope for than getting along with Derrick just about like before? Derrick was afraid of relationships then, and she was certain he was still afraid of relationships now.

"There's one more thing, Regina. You know I've been promising you a raise. Well, I'd say the time has come for me to keep my word. How does fifteen percent sound to you?"

Suddenly a light came on. "You had to give Derrick a big raise to get him back, didn't you?" she laughingly guessed.

"Well, I . . ."

"You were afraid I'd find out and let you have it right between the eyes!"

"Hey, that's not fair. I've promised you a raise for weeks now. Long before I got Derrick back onboard."

"But not before you knew you were going to try to get him back on board. Fifteen percent, you say? How much did you give Derrick?"

Clint's lip turned down as he shrugged. "A little more than that—maybe."

Reggie laughed and headed for the door. "Whatever you gave Derrick will do just fine for me," she said on the way out. Pausing at the door, she turned and gave him a wink. "And don't think I won't find out what that is. As you say, I'm the best investigator on the staff."

CHAPTER 3

It didn't take Reggie long to realize it was going to be like old times with Derrick. The first confrontation came over whose car they'd use to get to Falcon Field Airport. To her elation, she actually won! They drove her Pontiac Firebird while his precious Corvette sat all by itself in the agency parking lot. She wanted to jump up and shout her victory to the world, but decided that would be neither ladylike nor professional, so she enjoyed her triumph in silence. At the airport, it took only a few minutes to get the necessary clearance for the plane, which was kept fueled and ready to go at a moment's notice. The two of them were driven to the hangar in a small shuttle, where Derrick took over.

Reggie watched with quiet interest as Derrick painstakingly crossed off each item for his preflight check. When he started the engine, it coughed and caused the whole plane to shudder for an instant, then settled into a steady hum. "What did you do for a plane on the islands?" she asked curiously.

"The agency I worked for owned a Piper," he said, continuing his checks. "It wasn't as nice as this Cessna, but it got the job done."

Derrick picked up the radio mike and called the control tower. Once he received clearance, he shoved the throttle forward, revving the engine to taxi speed. As he released the brakes, the plane slowly moved forward toward the open hangar door. Within minutes, they were on the runway, where he lined the Cessna up for takeoff. After one more check with the tower, everything was ready to go.

Reggie adjusted the tension on her lap belt and drew an excited breath as Derrick moved the throttle open. The craft lurched forward, rapidly gaining speed until at last they were airborne. She watched the landscape shrink smaller and smaller as they ascended into the cloudless blue sky. It was breathtaking. Derrick put the plane into a slow, banking turn, taking them to a northerly heading. "So, where are you taking us?" she asked, having no idea what his plans were.

"I'd like to have a look at my dad's old mine," he answered without taking his eyes off the horizon. "I know it's a long shot, but I've always felt the investigation of the mine was sloppy, and I just want a look for myself."

Derrick was headed for the old mine? This brought a major question. "To the best of my knowledge, the mine is located somewhere in the middle of the pines near the Mogollon Rim. Where do you plan to land a Cessna in that country?"

"Dad constructed a landing strip near the mine."

"An old landing strip?" she asked nervously. "Is landing there safe? You're not going to get me killed, are you?"

Derrick smiled. "I've landed on that strip plenty of times, Regg. The way Dad built it, it'll be around long after you and I are both gone. But I'll take a hard look at it from the air before I set down."

Reggie wasn't as worried as she pretended. If there was one thing she knew about Derrick Beatty, it was that he never took unnecessary chances. Sometimes he was cautious to a fault—to her way of thinking. Between the two of them, she was the one who liked to live on the edge. His cautious attitude went way beyond the way he flew airplanes. It even extended to the way he treated friendships with the opposite gender. She had no idea what it would ever take to loosen him up, but whatever it was, it had eluded her throughout the years of their friendship. She was amazed that a woman like Brandilynne could come as close to pulling Derrick in as she did, and she was anything but surprised when that one fell through the cracks.

"The last time I was here was about two weeks before Dad vanished," Derrick explained. "We flew up in his old biplane." Derrick glanced over at Reggie. "You *do* remember that old plane, right?"

"How could anyone forget your dad's old yellow biplane? I think he gave every kid in town a ride in it at one time or another. I got my share of rides during my school years. It was a kick, for sure."

"I loved that old bird." Derrick grinned. "Dad bought it the year I was born."

"What was it—some sort of military plane?" Reggie asked.

"Yeah, it was, as a matter of fact. It was the last biplane the military ever used—an N3N-3. Its primary use was as a navy trainer during World War II. Dad did all the work restoring it himself. He kept it in tip-top shape to the very end."

The very end . . . ? These words hit Reggie like a cold slap in the face. "Are you hinting you think your dad crashed the old plane in the ocean like so many other people believe?" she asked soberly.

"No! Dad was too cautious a pilot to take the old plane over the ocean without filing a flight plan first. And as far as the suicide hypothesis goes, that's totally preposterous. Anyone who knew Dad would know that he would never take his own life."

Reggie had become somewhat acquainted with Samuel when he served as bishop during her teenage years, and she knew him a little better because of her association with Derrick. Of course, there weren't many in those parts who didn't know *of* Samuel Beatty; he was more or less a local legend. His greatest fame came through the stories of his gold mining days, although many remembered him as the one who envisioned and constructed The Majestic Saguaro Resort in the White Mountains of Arizona.

Even though Samuel was the one behind building the resort, it was Derrick's brother, Corbin, who was there to turn the key on opening day. To Reggie, it was always a big part of the mystery why Samuel had deeded the resort to Corbin instead of Derrick. She, along with several others, had done their best to convince Derrick to contest the will that showed up out of nowhere immediately following Samuel's disappearance. But Derrick flatly refused to be party to anything that might blacken the memory of his father's name.

Reggie had mixed emotions about his refusal. Part of her wanted Derrick to fight for his rights while another part of her wanted to respect Derrick's wishes. She often wondered how much this all had to do with Derrick's going away less than six months after the resort opened to the public.

Forcing her thoughts back to the present, she asked a question about Herb Solomon, Samuel's partner during his gold mining days. "When you flew up here with your father that day, did it have anything to do with Herb wanting to reopen the mine?"

"It had everything to do with it," Derrick affirmed. "Herb had it in his head there was another vein rich enough to go after, but he needed Dad's expertise to evaluate the vein's true worth. Dad intended to take a look at it that morning and invited me to tag along."

Reggie already knew the part of the story about Herb Solomon wanting to reopen the mine. When Samuel closed down operation to pursue his dream of building the resort, it left Herb without an income. Even though Herb was a full partner in the mine, he had nothing to do with the mining itself. Herb had bought into the partnership by financing Samuel when he discovered the gold, but he didn't have the personal funds to set up the operation. In the ensuing years, Herb ran into some bad luck and ended up heavily dependent on the mine for his income. Since Samuel had a master's degree in geology, Herb trusted his judgement on the value of the new vein. It was common knowledge that Herb had asked for Samuel's help in evaluating any new vein that might have come under question, but no one ever seemed to know what came of Herb's request. This included Reggie, although she did know Herb never restarted the mining operation. Instead, he went to work for Corbin once the resort opened. "So did your dad check out the new vein that day?" she asked.

"Nope. It never happened. We no sooner got the old biplane on the ground than a huge thunderstorm hit. And I do mean huge." Derrick laughed. "It dumped a ton of water on us. We threw a tarp over the open seats and took cover under it as best we could. I was about ready to change my name to Noah before that one blew over. By the time we got the tarp folded and stored back in the plane, the sun was breaking through the clouds with a beauty that took our breath away. You know what a nature lover Dad was."

Reggie smiled at her memory of the man. "I'll bet he wanted to go for a trek in the forest, since it's a whole new world after a big storm."

Derrick nodded. "You got that right. We hiked all the way up to Butterfly Falls and back. By then, he was out of the mood to go traipsing through an old mine, so we climbed in the plane and spent the rest of the day up with the eagles." Derrick sighed. "That is one great memory, Regg. Whenever I remember Dad, I think of that day."

As Reggie considered these things, she contemplated whether she should approach an old subject she had never been able to break down Derrick's resistance to. Even though she never really knew Corbin, she did know he and Derrick were fraternal twins. She also knew there had been a falling-out between the two brothers. On more than one occasion when she and Derrick had worked together in the past, she had tried without success to learn what caused the rift. Whatever it was,

Derrick refused to talk about it. Reggie hoped that perhaps in the four and a half years he had been away, he had undergone an attitude change about the subject. *Nothing ventured, nothing gained,* she thought. "Speaking of your family," she said, trying to ease into the subject. "What do you hear from your brother?"

Judging from Derrick's reaction—a tighter grip on the controls and an icy frown filling his face—Reggie knew instantly there had been no attitude change. "I haven't heard anything from Corbin," he bluntly stated. "The two of us haven't spoken in years. You should know that, Regg."

"Oh, that's right," she fibbed. "I'd forgotten. I'm sure you told me what caused the trouble between you and him, but I've forgotten that too. Care to refresh my memory?"

Derrick shook his head and actually managed a slight laugh. "Nice try, Regg, but no brass ring. That's part of my past I don't even think of, let alone talk about."

"Oh, come on, Derrick!" she pressed. "This is me you're talking to—your old friend and partner. What happened between you and Corbin? Was it over a girl?"

"Regg! So help me if you don't drop it I'm going to push you out of this plane."

"I knew it—it *was* over a girl. And one of these days I'm going to find out what her name was."

"Regg!"

"Okay, okay! I'll drop it." She grinned, then added, "But you could at least tell me if she was pretty."

"I'll tell you what's pretty," he said in an obvious move to change the subject. "Those mountains down there. Now that's a beauty you can write home about. Someday I'm going to own a house right in the middle of all this."

Reggie toyed with the idea of telling him he could have had an entire resort if he'd only taken pains to contest the will his brother had dragged out of nowhere, but she thought better of it. For the next few minutes, they both remained in their own silent thoughts until Derrick at last pointed out the airstrip. "There it is!" he exclaimed. "I'll drop down a few hundred feet and do a flyby to see what it looks like."

Reggie felt a rush as he brought the plane down until they were barely over the treetops. She loved it. "Everything looks great," Derrick observed. "Hang on while I set us down."

It was only a short walk from the airstrip to the entrance of the old mine. Reggie had never seen the mine, but she recognized it from newspaper articles and television reports. The place had been cordoned off with a twelve-foot-high fence topped with razor wire. The one gate was secured with a lock and chain. "Who's responsible for this now?" she asked, realizing someone had to be in charge of security for the place, but not knowing who it might be with Samuel out of the picture.

"It's Corbin's responsibility," Derrick explained. "The mine and resort together make up the Beatty Enterprises. When he inherited it, the mine came with it."

Reggie glanced around. "Do you think he'd be satisfied with just this fence for security? That resort must've made him a wealthy man, and he could be the target of a healthy lawsuit if someone got themselves hurt here at the old mine."

"Good point, Regg. He could have someone watching the place, or maybe some hidden surveillance cameras. I wouldn't put it past him."

Reggie couldn't help the uneasy feeling that crept over her. "Maybe we should have asked our legal department to apply for a search warrant before we came up here," she suggested. "We could be sticking our necks out."

"If we did that, my brother would have pulled in his own high-powered lawyers, and things could have been tied up in court for no telling how long. I want to see inside that mine now."

"Okay," she agreed. "We'll throw caution to the wind. You want to pick that lock, or shall I do it?"

This caused Derrick to grin. "I'd better do it," he teased. "We might be up here all day if we have to wait while you pick it."

"You think you're funny, don't you?" she rebutted. "I could probably pick that lock in half the time it'll take you."

Now Derrick laughed out loud. " 'Anything you can do, I can do better?' Isn't that the way the old song goes?"

"Just open the lock and forget about singing," she said. "Neither one of us could carry a tune in a milk bucket." Reggie watched as Derrick removed his lock-picking tools from a pouch in his pocket and made short work of the lock. She wouldn't admit it, but it would have taken her quite a bit longer. Picking locks wasn't among her greater skills.

Derrick pushed on the gate. It opened with a rusty groan. They stepped inside to face a gaping hole in the side of the mountain where a set of time-worn iron rails vanished ghostlike into the forbidding darkness. A coldness gripped Reggie as she pondered what might be waiting inside that blackness. She could tolerate almost anything except the possibility of rats. Rats were one thing Reggie hated. "Are you sure this is safe?" she questioned, trying hard not to show her concern.

"We might run into a snake or two," Derrick replied knowingly. "But that's about it."

Snakes? Reggie reasoned to herself. That was something she hadn't thought about, but snakes were still better than rats. "What are we waiting for?" she stated boldly. "Let's check this place out."

She flipped on the five-cell flashlight Derrick had given her when they left the plane and shined it into the darkness. Using his own flashlight, Derrick stepped through the opening ahead of her. She hurriedly caught up. "Stay between the rails," he told her. "Walking is easier that way."

The more Reggie tried not to think about rats, the more squeamish she became. Every shadow took on the appearance of one of the furry little creatures just waiting to pounce at her. She remained very close to Derrick, hoping he wouldn't sense her apprehension. After a short time, they reached a large, hollowed-out room, which Derrick explained was where the mother lode had been extracted. "Not much to see in here," she remarked, shining her light around.

"It's just a played-out old mine, Regg. What did you expect?"

"I don't know. I've never been in a mine before."

"Well, so far I haven't spotted anything out of the ordinary."

"So is this it, then?" she asked, hoping he would confirm her guess.

"No, there's more. When the gold in this room played out, Dad drove a shaft straight back another hundred or so feet. I'll just tell you now that the going gets tougher from here."

Wonderful! she thought sarcastically. *Just what I was hoping for.*

Derrick led out again, this time through a smaller tunnel located at the rear of the room. There were no rails here, and the floor was much rougher than in the previous section. All at once, another fear crept into Reggie's consciousness. No longer was it just the rats. Now it was the overpowering feeling of claustrophobia. What in the world was Derrick thinking, dragging her into a place like this? What possible clue could this dingy old mine hold to Samuel's disappearance?

One step at a time, they inched forward. The air was stuffy here, and she noticed the shoring along the ceiling and walls was much closer in this part of the mine. Could this mean it was the weakest part? One more thing to think about.

From somewhere behind, the sound of a falling rock echoed through the darkness, causing her to lurch forward, grabbing Derrick by the arm. She heard him chuckle and felt a spike of anger at herself for her moment of weakness. But she didn't let go. Suddenly, Derrick stopped. "What the . . ." he gasped. "There's been a cave-in!"

Reggie peered around to see a pile of fallen rocks directly in their path. The tunnel was completely closed off from this point on. "I don't understand," Derrick said, examining it more closely. "This tunnel used to extend a good thirty feet farther. It took something pretty traumatic to cause this."

He bent down for a closer look. "Dynamite," he remarked. "There are powder marks here."

"An explosion?" she guessed.

"Yeah, a big one. I'd sure like to know when and how this happened. Dad would have mentioned something of this magnitude if he'd known."

"This could be significant," Reggie pondered aloud. "Something or someone might be buried behind this cave-in."

"My thoughts exactly," Derrick admitted.

"Is there a chance we could dig our way through the rubble to check it out?"

"Not with our bare hands. But we have cause for a warrant now. What we need is a crew up here with the right equipment."

Reggie could only guess what must have been going through Derrick's mind. Was his father's body buried behind this rubble? But if that were the case, what happened to his old biplane that vanished along with him?

Just then, a grapefruit-size rock dislodged from near the top of the rubble, brushing past Reggie's ankle as it rolled by. Letting out a scream, she threw both arms around Derrick's neck and hung on for dear life. It took less than a second to realize what she'd done. Feeling like a fool, she pulled back. "I—I'm sorry," she said. "I don't know what came over me."

She heard him quietly laugh, but he didn't voice an answer. Instead, he laid his flashlight aside and pulled out two items from a small case he had brought along. Reggie watched as he coated the area with a substance from a spray bottle, then shined a blue light on it. "Checking for blood?" she guessed.

"Yep. This is called a Luminol test. Something I picked up from one of the guys on Oahu who was skilled in forensic science. You spray the suspected area with Luminol, then shine a blue light on it, and any blood present will take on a glow."

"Like that glow right there?" Reggie asked, looking at what she reasoned were several places where rather large amounts of blood were indeed present.

"Exactly," Derrick explained. "There's blood splattered all over this place."

"This doesn't make sense, Derrick. If you found blood this easy, why wasn't it found in the initial investigation?"

"Darn good question, Regg. Like I've already mentioned, my feelings are that the initial investigation was a sham. I've always suspected Corbin had a part in keeping the whole picture from coming out. Give me a hand in gathering a few loose rocks with samples on them."

"You suspect it's your father's blood, don't you?" she asked.

"I'm not sure what I suspect, but I want a DNA test run on it."

"Do you have a sample of your father's DNA to compare it with?"

"No. But I can have it compared against my DNA. That'll put us in the ballpark."

Reggie considered this. "Even if it does compare favorably with yours, Derrick, who's to say it isn't your brother's?"

"You really believe in complicating things, don't you, Regg?"

"Just a thought."

"Okay, so we'll have to find a way to get a sample of Corbin's DNA. That should satisfy your argument."

"Yeah, right. You want to ask him for a sample, or shall I do it?"

Derrick just shook his head. "I'd say this finishes us up down here. How 'bout we get out of this place?"

Reggie gulped a breath of fresh air as Derrick closed the gate behind them and reattached the lock. She glanced at her watch to see it was just past noon. "I have a couple of granola bars in my purse," she noted. "Want to make a picnic out of this?"

"Why not?" he laughed. "Anything for a free lunch, especially when it's your treat."

"Where's this Butterfly Falls you mentioned going to with your dad?"

"It's not far. You up to a hike?"

"Yes, I'd like that. We'll have to go by the plane if you want that lunch, though. I left my purse there."

"It's on the way, and we need to drop off these samples and this equipment anyway."

"I'm sorry about what happened back there in the mine," she said as they walked. "I feel really dumb."

"Don't," Derrick soothed. "I grew up with that old mine, but it was a new experience for you." She smiled and was grateful he so graciously let it go at that.

At the plane, they dropped off the samples and equipment, and she grabbed them each a granola bar. "These might get a little dry without something to drink," she said.

"No problem. There's a stream not five minutes from here with the coldest and best water you ever tasted."

They headed off into the woods and, just as Derrick said, came to the stream in only a few minutes. By this time they had finished off the granola bars, and both were ready for a drink. Not waiting for Derrick, Reggie moved to the stream's edge, where she lay on her stomach and drew in a mouthful of the cold, delicious liquid. When she had drunk her fill, she stood to see Derrick on one knee scooping up the water with his hands. She broke out laughing. "You drink like a girl!" she teased. Then without thinking, she did something she instantly realized should never have been done. Placing a foot against his shoulder, she gave him a shove. He barely caught himself in time to keep from tumbling into the stream. Springing to his feet, he suddenly lunged for her, pushing her down on the soft grassy meadow and holding her there with one hand on each of her shoulders. She was laughing so hard it almost hurt. He was laughing too.

As the laughter died, she found herself looking up into those incredibly blue eyes with the sensation he was about to kiss her. Her pulse quickened, and she wished with all her heart he would kiss her. But after a long moment, he backed away and sat looking down at her. She eased herself up on one elbow and returned his look. He was the first to speak, catching her by complete surprise with his next words. "I see you're not wearing Walden's ring. I take it things didn't work out between you two?"

Reggie felt suddenly numb. She hadn't given a thought to Walden Stewart in the past four years. Walden wasn't a member of the Church, and if she had any thoughts of him ever converting, they failed to materialize. Reggie never once held any serious thoughts about marrying Walden, and hard as it was for her to admit, she accepted his ring only because she hoped it might make Derrick jealous enough to stand up for his own rights. It might have worked, too, if it hadn't been for that pushy Brandilynne McDowell and the fact that Derrick's dad had just dropped off the edge of the earth. All this combined had apparently been too much for Derrick to handle, and that's when he ran off to the islands. "What business is it of yours if things didn't work out between Walden and me?" she stated sarcastically. "That's getting a little personal isn't it?"

"About as personal as asking what happened between Corbin and me, wouldn't you think?"

Reggie felt the wind leave her sails. Darn this man anyway! He always had a way of turning things around on her. Sometimes she almost wished she could hate him. She eased up to her feet. "Walden was a nice enough guy," she said. "The chemistry just wasn't there."

Derrick stood. "I could have told you that if you'd asked. When your Mr. Right comes along, he'll be someone who's temple worthy."

She could still feel her pulse throbbing in her throat. "Just as your Miss Right will be," she remarked. She wanted to add the little fact that Brandilynne wasn't temple worthy either, but she didn't. She was proud of herself for this until Derrick's next cutting remark.

"Yeah. You suppose you might consider being her maid of honor?"

Reggie saw red. Never in her life had she wanted to hit someone more than she wanted to hit Derrick now. She fought to contain her emotions and hoped he wouldn't notice. "No!" she countered. "I plan on being your best man!"

This sent Derrick into another burst of laughter. When he settled again, he said something that really caught her interest. "If I ever do propose, I'm going to do it right here on this very spot."

"What?" she gasped. "Why, pray tell?"

"I don't know." He shrugged. "It just seems like a good spot. For one thing, the ground is soft enough not to hurt my knees."

"You plan on kneeling?" she giggled. "A bit old-fashioned, wouldn't you say?"

"Hey, I'm an old-fashioned sort of guy. Come on, the falls are just ahead. You won't believe your eyes when you see them." He offered her an arm, which she ached to accept. Instead, she just pretended he was joking and started off in the direction the stream was flowing, realizing this would have to take her to the falls. Derrick caught up.

Within minutes, they reached one of the most beautiful sights Reggie had ever seen. With the roar of the falls in her ears, she moved out on the ledge overlooking them. The water plummeted an estimated two hundred feet, crashing to the rocky bottom with a force that created a milky mist. Sunlight filtering through the dense trees played against the mist in such a way as to create a nearly perfect rainbow, its colors so brilliant it almost took Reggie's breath away. Instinctively, she edged farther out on the ledge for a better look.

"Careful!" Derrick warned. "Not too near the edge. It's slippery and dangerous."

"You worry too much," she countered. "Take a lesson in relaxation from an expert."

Derrick reached for her hand and gently pulled her back a step. "The view is just as spectacular from here," he said softly. "And it's a whole lot safer."

Reggie didn't oppose him, figuring it wasn't worth arguing over. And besides, he was right about the view being just as spectacular. "So, where do we go from here?" she asked. When he didn't answer right away, she glanced to see a puzzled look on his face. She instantly realized he must have misunderstood what she meant with her question. He thought she was asking about their personal relationship.

"In our investigation, I mean," she hurriedly specified. "We've done about all we can here for now. What's next?"

She wasn't sure, but she almost thought his expression hinted at disappointment. "I thought we might take a look at The Majestic Saguaro Resort," he explained. "I've never seen the place since it opened to the public."

Reggie was aware that Derrick had been in on quite a bit of the planning when Samuel was developing the resort, and she had always assumed that after his father's mysterious death, Derrick had purposely avoided the grand opening. His statement about never seeing the place since it opened confirmed this. Reggie had never seen the resort either. "You're talking about seeing it from the air, I presume?" she asked.

He nodded. "Probably. We'll play it by ear. If a reason for a closer look comes along, we'll discuss our possibilities then. Come on, let's get back to the plane."

CHAPTER 4

The flight from the mine to the resort took about fifteen minutes. The first thing visible was the lodge itself. Reggie caught her breath at the sight of it. What she saw put the TV images of the place to shame. This was a true Cinderella's castle if she'd ever envisioned one. "How tall is it?" she asked.

"Seven stories. And if you think the outside is spectacular, you should look at the suites sometime. Dad designed them all himself, if that tells you anything."

"What would it be like?" Reggie sighed. "They're probably something I'll never see."

Derrick laughed. "You mean Walden never took you there for a weekend?"

"Will you get off the subject of Walden!" she snapped. "That's ancient history!"

Derrick glanced over at her. "Any new boyfriends to take his place?"

"That's none of your business!"

"It might be," he persisted. "I could take a look at the guy and see if he's good enough for you. I'd hate to see you waste time on another Walden." Before a fuming Reggie could retaliate, Derrick pointed out the window. "Get a load of that golf course, Regg. Now that the grass has matured, it's more incredible than when Dad put it in."

Reggie bit her lip and wished for something clever to say, but nothing came to mind. How could she ever have been so blind as to think she might actually have feelings for this man? "Golf's not my game," she responded. She rolled her eyes, remembering that she had wanted to say something clever. Why had that stupid remark come out?

"I didn't say golf was your game, Regg. I don't like golf either. But you have to admit, that course is pretty spectacular."

She glanced back at the course. Derrick was right, of course. It was spectacular. Then, a little farther ahead of them, she noticed something else. "There," she said, pointing at the tennis courts. "That's a real game." This brought a smile to her lips as she remembered how hard Derrick used to try to stay with her on a tennis court. She had been women's champion all four years in college. Derrick never once could best her at that game.

He smiled. "You still as good at it as you used to be?" he asked.

"Better," she bragged through a huge grin.

"You'll have to give me the pleasure of a rematch sometime. I tuned up my game on the islands."

"Anytime, Derrick Beatty! In fact, if you'll set this plane down, I'll take you on right now."

"I could do that, but I doubt the resort owner would lay out a velvet carpet for us."

Reggie strongly considered her next remark before venturing into it, but decided to throw caution aside. "Those could've been your courts, you know—if you'd contested your brother's version of your father's will."

Derrick rolled his eyes. "What would I do with a multi-million-dollar resort?"

Reggie knew this was a good time to shut up, but she was still fuming from his remarks about her supposed "boyfriends." "What would you do with it? If you owned that resort, I'm sure you could find some woman dumb enough to marry you for your money, and you'd live happily ever after."

This brought a chuckle as he glanced over at her. "Do you really think there's a woman out there dumb enough to marry me?"

"Probably not," she said, doing her best to hold a straight face. "You had your chance with Miss McDowell if you remember, and you blew it." It was the first time she had actually mentioned Brandilynne's name to him, and the startled look on his face made her effort at not laughing a losing battle. To her surprise, Derrick soon joined in. Reggie had to admit, it was nice to know he could laugh about Brandilynne. And she also had to admit it was no use trying to stay mad at him. She caught her breath, wiped her eyes, and glanced back at the resort. "Your dad thought of everything, didn't he? Riding stables, dinner cruises, a village of quaint little shops. There's not much missing."

"Only one thing," Derrick corrected her. "Dad should be down there enjoying it now."

This statement sobered things up. Reggie's thoughts returned to the business at hand. "Speaking of your father, what did you expect to find here that might help in revisiting his disappearance?"

"I don't know, Regg. We have virtually no evidence to go on. Maybe I'm just grasping for straws. Or maybe I just wanted to get a firsthand look at the place."

"Didn't your dad's vision include an island in the center of his man-made lake?" she asked.

"Yeah, a small one. He wanted to turn it into a tropical restaurant, although that wasn't something he planned for the first stage of development. He figured he could add that little touch later on. As long as we're here, we might as well have a look at the island. It's only a couple of minutes from here in the Cessna."

Derrick turned the plane to the west, where the silhouette of palm trees soon became visible against the afternoon sun. As they flew nearer, Reggie could see the island was covered with vegetation and had a well-cared-for look about it. There was no sign of a restaurant under construction, but there was one small house clearly visible. Derrick noticed it about the same time she did.

"I wonder what that's all about," he remarked. "It wasn't part of the original plan to put a house on the island. Hang on, Regg. I'm going to fly in for a closer look."

"The place looks lived-in," Reggie remarked as they flew by. "Curtains in the windows, flower gardens, a rocker on the porch. All the signs are there."

"Yeah," Derrick agreed. "Someone lives there all right. Probably a caretaker for the island."

"You think?"

"Well, look at the condition of the island, Regg. Someone's looking out for it with tender loving care. It just figures the guy would live here."

"If that's the case, where's his boat?" Reggie asked. "I see a boat dock, but no boat."

"He's probably on the mainland," Derrick guessed. Then, with a boyish grin, he added, "Too bad this Cessna requires such a long strip to take off and land. If we were in my dad's old biplane, we could set down and look the place over with the occupant gone."

"I don't see any airstrip," Reggie remarked, looking the small island over from end to end.

"There's no landing strip, but the west shore is hard packed enough that Dad could land the old biplane there, which he did several times. But, like I say, it's not good enough to land a Cessna on."

Derrick throttled forward and pulled back on the controls, returning the plane to cruising altitude. "I suppose that's about all the good we can do here," he acknowledged. "I guess I'll head back in unless you have any suggestions I haven't thought of while we have the Cessna." She didn't.

On the flight home, she mulled over what it had been like working with Derrick on his first day back. She had to admit, it wasn't all that bad. After securing the plane, they started back to the office. Even though it was too late to get anything else done for the day, Reggie needed to drop Derrick off to get his car. She was surprised when he asked her to detour by the Pointe at South Mountain, where he bought dinner. It made for an especially nice evening and brought back memories of times they had gone out for dinners in the past.

That night, Reggie lay awake thinking a very long time before sleep caught up to her. Why did it have to be Derrick Beatty who made her feel this way? There were dozens of other wonderful LDS men, some of whom she dated frequently, but none of whom made her heart sing like Derrick. She didn't know who she was the most angry with—Derrick for coming home to disrupt her life again, or herself for allowing him to do it. And to top it off, it seemed like salt in a wound that he had the nerve to invade her dreams that night.

CHAPTER 5

Corbin Beatty pulled out a chair and sat down for breakfast at his private, poolside table. A confirmed man of habit, Corbin always started his day with the same menu: three eggs, a large cut of ham, two slices of wheat toast covered with grape jam, and a cup of steaming hot black coffee. Sometimes it made him angry that after all these years, he still felt a hint of guilt for the coffee or occasional glass of wine he allowed himself to indulge in. Corbin had put the teachings of his confining childhood religion behind him many years ago, and he had learned to enjoy the freedom that came from being his own man. But there were still those rare moments when a quiet little voice would whisper words of reproach in his ear.

Reaching for a napkin, he was interrupted by the ringing of his cell phone. A glance at the ID told him it was Brandy Carrol, the resort office manager. He pressed the receive button. "Morning, Brandy. What's going on?"

"If you have a minute, I'd like you to stop by my office, Mr. Beatty. Officer Pat Michaels from security is here with something I think you should personally attend to."

Corbin threw the napkin on the table. He knew Brandy well enough to know she wouldn't interrupt him unless it was for something she considered important. "Can you give me a hint over the phone, or is it too delicate?" he asked.

"I'd rather you hear it firsthand," she responded. "I'll let you be the judge of how delicate it is. I will tell you this much: it concerns your brother."

"My brother?" Corbin repeated suspiciously, his mind racing for a possible reason why security could be concerned about Derrick. Whatever the reason, it was important he handle it now. "I'll be right there, Brandy. Make sure Pat waits for me."

Corbin shut off his phone and slid it into his shirt pocket. He stood, then picked up a slice of toast as if to take a bite. He paused in thought, still struggling for answers about this strange turn of events. He and Derrick hadn't spoken in more years than he could remember, and the last he had heard, Derrick had taken up residence somewhere in the Hawaiian Islands. Corbin had no idea why Derrick had done this, but he was glad. The greater the distance between them, the better—for more than one reason.

Dropping the uneaten toast back on his plate, Corbin headed for the lodge. He took the elevator to the third floor and quickly made his way to Brandy's office, where he spotted Officer Michaels. "What's this all about, Pat?" he asked.

The officer handed over a stack of photographs. "When I showed these to Brandy, she felt you should see them," he explained.

Corbin felt his pulse quicken as he glanced at the first one. It was Derrick all right, and the woman with him was once his partner at the detective agency where Derrick used to work. "What is this?" Corbin barked, quickly thumbing through the rest of the stack. "Why were they snooping around the old mine?"

After a moment, he lowered the photographs to stare at Officer Michaels. "When were these taken?" he demanded.

"Early yesterday afternoon," the officer replied. "On Herb Solomon's orders, I send someone up to the mine periodically, just to make sure everything is in order. Yesterday it was Ryan

Timmerman. Ryan spotted a Cessna circling suspiciously around the old airstrip, so he stayed out of sight and watched. His suspicions proved sound when the plane landed and these two emerged. He snapped these pictures with a telephoto lens."

Anger gripped Corbin as he pondered what this might mean. Corbin hated the mine and would have disposed of it long ago if he hadn't feared doing so might call attention to the place, possibly allowing someone to stumble onto the secret buried inside. Not that this was likely, since it would require someone who knew exactly what they were looking for—and that wasn't apt to happen. After carefully considering his options and reasoning out the possible consequences of each, Corbin concluded his best course of action would be to seal off the old mine and allow the publicity surrounding the place to gradually die out. As an added precaution, he placed Herb Solomon in charge of security for the mine. This posed no risk since Herb already knew the secret. Up until now, everything had gone according to plan. Time had erased the curiosity of the mine from most everyone's mind. But Derrick's entering the picture was another matter altogether. If there was anyone who might uncover the dreaded secret, it was Derrick. All this raced through Corbin's mind as he pressed on with this conversation. "Did your man get close enough to hear any of their conversation, Pat?" he asked.

"No. He purposely stayed out of sight, since Herb has ordered us to never put any of our men in danger at the mine. Ryan did exactly as he was told. He took pictures and reported back to me right away. I'd have said something sooner, but I wanted to get the pictures developed first."

Corbin removed a handkerchief from his pocket and wiped his brow. He'd always feared Derrick might come back to haunt him someday, especially after Corbin had so skillfully excluded Derrick from their father's will. But Corbin wouldn't let Derrick get away with anything—especially if it involved the mine.

Derrick was a weak fool who had never been a match for Corbin's superiority. The only reason Samuel ever favored Derrick over Corbin was because Derrick went along with the old man's fanaticism about religion. Corbin had always reasoned that the Mormon Church was just an albatross around their father's neck, and Derrick didn't have sense enough to see that.

"Is Herb aware of this yet, Pat?" Corbin asked sharply.

"Not yet. I came by Brandy's desk hoping she might know where to reach him. It was her idea to contact you first."

"You did right. But I want Herb brought in on this right away. And I want security posted at the old mine twenty-four hours a day. One more thing, Brandy. Call our law firm and see what legal recourse we have against these two for breaking into the mine. Let me know what you find out."

All thoughts of breakfast had disappeared by now. It seemed the day Corbin had long feared might just be here. But, he figured, if it was war Derrick wanted, then it was war Derrick would have—a war that would be fought and won on Corbin's turf.

Wanting to be alone, Corbin left the lodge and headed for the lake, where he pulled off his shoes and strolled barefoot along the sandy beach. A gentle breeze brushed his face with a touch of coolness that brought a welcome relief to the hot days of summer just now beginning to ease into a late autumn. Staring out across the lake, he drew in a deep breath. It felt good knowing all this was his. Who would ever have imagined that he, the prodigal son of the family, would one day rise to such heights? The thrill of it all was nearly intoxicating, at least until his thoughts drifted to the subject of his mother. No man ever loved a mother more than Corbin loved his. Her death was the greatest tragedy of his life.

Spotting a small, flat rock near his feet, Corbin bent down and picked it up. Feeling its smoothness between his fingers, he remembered how his mother used to refer to Derrick as being firm like a rock. She was always proud of Derrick. In her eyes,

Derrick could do no wrong. Corbin had craved for a way to make her just as proud of him, but the only thing she ever wanted had to do with that church.

Giving the stone a toss, Corbin watched as it skipped four times over the surface of the lake before sinking out of sight. He wondered if his mother would be proud of him now. Any mother should be proud of a son with power and wealth like Corbin enjoyed now. But in his heart, he realized this was a lie. Evelana Beatty was a woman who would have been proud to see Corbin serve a mission in some offbeat place, then settle down into an honorable occupation—even if it paid next to nothing—just as long as he gave ten percent of his income to the church she loved more than her own life. No, regardless of his financial accomplishments, Evelana Beatty still wouldn't be proud. She'd continue to love him, but she wouldn't be proud. Much as he tried to downplay this, there was no way to rid the truth of its sadness, nor was there a way to wash away the guilt that always accompanied these feelings whenever Corbin let them in. Corbin tried to tell himself it didn't matter, but knew that he would still be lying to himself. Someday, he was going to construct a monument to his mother's name, but for now there were more timely matters to consider—like why his brother and that woman detective were snooping around the old mine.

CHAPTER 6

Derrick was out of bed at the earliest glimpse of daylight and was the first one to the office. When there was work to be done, he wasn't one to put it off. Picking up the phone on his desk, he made a call. "Sheriff Quinn's office," came the answer in a lovely feminine voice.

"Officer Brenda Rossland, I assume," Derrick responded. Derrick knew Officer Rossland had been Quinn's personal receptionist for years, and he recognized her voice now.

"This is Brenda. And you are . . ."

"You have to ask, Brenda? I'm crushed. I thought you might remember me."

"Derrick Beatty?" she guessed. "Is it you?"

"In the flesh."

"Well, I'll be! I figured someone would have shot you by now," she jested. "Is this a long-distance call, or have you graced our town with a visit?"

"Neither," he laughed. "I've come home to haunt you, Brenda."

"You're home? On the level? Why didn't you notify me? I'd have baked you a cake or something."

"I'm holding you to a rain check on that, Brenda. I remember how your pineapple upside-down cake melts in the mouth. Is your boss in, by chance?" Derrick asked, referring to Sheriff Quinn.

Brenda laughed. "Ed left word for me to hold all calls as he's on a hot project. But I suspect he'll make an exception when I tell him you're on the line. I'm going to put you on hold, okay?"

After a couple of minutes, another familiar voice came on the line. "Derrick Beatty? Is it really you, or is Brenda playing games with this old sheriff?"

"It's me, Ed," Derrick chuckled. "So what's the hot case you're on? Anything the best PI you ever worked with can help out on?"

"It's a drug bust we're closing in on. I think we have everything in hand, but just in case any of them slip through my fingers, I'll keep you in mind. So, I take it you're back in the PI business here again?"

"Clint reinstated me to my old job."

"Oh, yeah? Should I have the wife start looking for something suitable for a wedding gift?"

Derrick rolled his eyes. "Referring to Regg and me, I presume?"

"Everyone knows you two are a match made in heaven, Derrick. Everyone but you and Regg. I think I'll give some thought to arresting the two of you and locking you up in the same cell. The way I see it, you'll either kill each other, or you'll break down and propose to the lady."

"Yeah, yeah, yeah! Like Regg would ever say yes to a loser like me even if I did humiliate myself by proposing. You will pardon me if I turn the subject to the point I called about. It concerns my dad."

"What about your dad?" the sheriff asked, his voice abruptly more serious.

"I'm doing some investigating into his disappearance, Ed. I was up at the old mine yesterday, and I found some interesting things. Were you in charge of investigating the mine back when this all started?"

"I sent a couple of guys up there, yeah. They ran into problems when they found the place under private investigation by a firm hired by your brother, Corbin. They were able to do some checking, but not as detailed as I would have liked. Problem was, Corbin's lawyers got a judge to back up the private investigation and shove my men to the background."

"I've always had a hunch the mine was never detailed the way it should have been, and guess what, Ed? I have proof of my hunch now."

"You what?"

"I was up there yesterday, Ed. I found evidence of an explosion that's closed off several feet of mine. And that's not all. I also found traces of blood. Lots of it."

"Cave-in? Blood? Something's rotten in Denmark, Derrick. Those private people must have had more cover-up in mind than looking for real evidence."

"Either that or they weren't experienced in forensics. Someone had done a good job cleaning up the mess. I only found it with a Luminol test."

Quinn grew silent a moment or so. "Blood, you say? And you have samples?"

"I do. And I'm asking you to order a DNA test to see if any of it compares with mine."

"Trying to link the blood to your dad?"

"Yeah."

"We can do that, Derrick. Now, tell me about this part of the mine you found closed off. Do you think a body could be concealed in there?"

"It's not something I'm hoping for, Ed. But it *is* a definite possibility. Dad has to be someplace. I need your help. Can you get a warrant and send someone up there to open it up?"

"Consider it done, Derrick. And I need those samples ASAP."

"I have them here at the office. Can you send someone to pick them up?"

"I can do that. Your dad and I go way back, Derrick. Nothing would make me happier than to bring some closure to his case."

"You know my brother will oppose you checking the mine. And you also know he has an army of lawyers on his side."

"As evidenced by his ability to keep the original investigation in private hands? I think with the ammunition we have now, a judge will take a different view. Give me a week and I'll have your warrant."

"Thanks, Ed. And keep me posted, will you?"

"Do you have to ask?"

Derrick hung up the phone just as Clint entered the office. "I see you're at it early," Clint remarked when he spotted Derrick. "So, how did your first day back with Regina go? Pleasant, I hope?"

Derrick shook his head. "What it is with you, Clint? You don't ask what I might have dug up my first day back; you ask how it went with Regg. We're just two PIs who happen to make a great team. Why does everyone want to make more of it than that?"

"Okay, okay, so hold your cool, pal. What sort of stuff did you dig out?"

Derrick pointed to a box on his desk containing the rocks with blood samples on them. "Regg and I went up to my dad's old mine," he explained. "We found some things that definitely need checking into, including the blood on these rocks."

Clint glanced at the rocks, which to the naked eye didn't show traces of red. "I take it you used some forensic technique to prove the blood is there?"

"It's there, Clint, believe me. Sheriff Quinn has someone coming by to pick this up. If they come while I'm out, will you see to it the stuff gets into their hands?"

"Will do. So, what's on your agenda for today?"

"For one thing, I plan on dropping by Chandler law firm. They're the ones who handled my dad's probate. I'd like a look at the alleged will and any other papers they may have socked away. I know everything appeared to be on the up and up at the time of the hearing, but I'd like a look at it myself."

"It's about time you took an interest in your dad's will. If you think back, there were any number of us urging you to shove your nose into things at the time of the probate."

"Okay, I admit I made a mistake. But at the time, I had other things on my mind."

The office door opened, and Derrick looked up to see Reggie step through it. He did a double take. She was wearing a blue pantsuit that looked new, and her hair shone like he never remembered seeing it. He couldn't take his eyes off her.

Clint quickly excused himself and vanished into his inner office, leaving Derrick and Reggie alone in the outer office. "You're up early," she said. "I figured after the meal you put away last night, you might need to sleep it off this morning."

"You know me," he countered, trying not to let his interest in her appearance show. "Up in the morning, out on the job. That sort of thing. Now that you're here, I'd like to make a stop by a certain law firm. Or do you have some catching up to do before leaving the office?"

"Clint pulled everything off my plate so I could help with your investigation," she explained. "I'm ready when you are."

"Great!" He smiled. "We'll take my car."

CHAPTER 7

Amos Shepard held the rod high over his head and, with pointed skill, let the line fly. With perfect satisfaction he observed the little red bobber fall lightly to the lake. Leaning back on his favorite rock, he watched the ripples drift away from the bobber until they eventually melted into the calmness of the water's surface. Amos loved fishing at the time of day when the sun was hanging lazily in the morning sky. Suddenly, just to his right, a large green frog appeared at the water's edge. In two hops, the frog was on the dry sand, staring up at his human company with fearless eyes.

"Well, hello there, my friend," Amos said to the frog. "It's been a couple of days since I saw you last. Where have you been? Ah, let me guess. You probably ran across some cute little number with big dreamy eyes, right? You've been courting, haven't you pal?"

"Burr-ock!" the frog croaked.

"Yeah," Amos laughed. "I thought so. Nothing wrong with a fellow doing a bit of courting now and then." He pulled a toothpick from his shirt pocket, then bit down on it and looked off at nowhere in particular. "Funny, isn't it, my friend?" he said at length. "What some folks would give for the kind of life you and I share on this island. Not me, though. Sometimes I think it might be worth the risk I'd be taking to get off this island. Maybe I could learn to really start living again."

The frog took one short hop closer to Amos, and if frogs could smile, this one most certainly did. "Yeah I know," Amos chuckled. "You like it here. And that's okay for a frog. Me, I'd like a bit of a change." Pulling the toothpick from his mouth, Amos stared at the tip of it for a long time. "I stand accused of killing a man, pal," he explained as he had done so many times before. "His name was Samuel Beatty. Yeah, I know you've heard this story before. But I just feel like talking about it, okay?"

"Burr-ock!" the frog croaked once more.

"Worst part is, I didn't even know the man. I can't remember a thing about the foul deed, pal. I guess I was in a pretty bad way at the time. Old Herb Solomon tells me that was the case anyhow. Herb's my best friend, you know. He's been watching out for me a long time now, letting me stay here on this island and all. Herb doesn't own the island. A fellow named Corbin Beatty owns it. Herb works for Corbin as a facilities manager. The upkeep of this island is actually Herb's responsibility, but he leaves it all to me. Oh, he checks on me now and again, but he doesn't bother my routine any. I think he's satisfied with the way I do things. I suspect Corbin Beatty is beholding to me, anyway. They tell me the man I killed was his dad, but he and Corbin never got along all that great. The way I see it, Corbin was probably glad when I got his old man out of the way and put the resort into his greedy hands. What do you think, my friend? Do you agree with me?"

The frog took one last hop. This time he landed at the edge of Amos's foot with his chin resting on the man's shoe. "Yeah, you agree with me, all right. But there's not one darn thing you can do about it any more than I can." Amos reached down and stroked the frog's back. "Feels good, don't it, pal? Everyone deserves to have their back rubbed once in a while."

Just then, the sound of an approaching boat caught Amos's ear. He glanced up. "Well what do you know, friend? We were just talking about old Herb, and guess who's about to pay me a visit? Excuse me, pal," he said, reeling in his line and laying the pole down. "I need to see what old Herb has on his mind."

As the boat pulled up to the wooden dock, the frog made a hasty retreat. Herb Solomon climbed out and attached a mooring line. "Good morning, Amos," he said. "How's it going, buddy?"

Amos shrugged. "Going as good as it can for a man in my predicament. So, what's up with you?"

"Nothing much. I'm going to be pretty tied up the next little while on a business matter that's just been brought to my attention, and I wanted to check on you before I dove in. Do you need anything from the mainland?"

"I could use some fuel for my generator. I have plenty for a day or so, but that's about it."

"I'll have some sent out, Amos. You doing okay in the food department? Need anything there?"

"Groceries have been arriving twice a week like always. You take good care of me, Herb. I hope you never end up in trouble with the law over this."

"Put that out of your mind, Amos. If push ever comes to shove, Corbin's lawyers will come to my rescue."

"I guess I should count myself lucky for Corbin's lawyers. Life is a lot better on this island than it would be in a prison cell, eh, Herb?"

"Yeah, Amos. A lot better. Look, I gotta be going. Anything you need, get a message to me through whoever makes your deliveries. Anything, Amos. You know I mean that."

"I know, Herb. Thanks."

* * *

Herb wet his lips and untied the mooring line. He wished with every inch of his soul he could do more for his friend, but he knew that was impossible under the circumstances. "It might

be a couple of weeks before I get back out here, Amos. This item
of business I mentioned may take awhile to clear up."

The "item of business," as he called it, was one Herb had
hoped would never have to be faced. Herb had always liked
Derrick Beatty and had known from the beginning how Derrick
was cheated by Samuel's supposedly authentic will. Herb was one
of only two men (not counting a certain unscrupulous doctor)
who knew the truth about Samuel and his estate. The other was
Corbin Beatty, a man Herb neither liked nor trusted, but one
whom Herb remained indebted to so deeply he was sure he could
never pull free of the man's web without completely ruining his
own life in the process. Tossing the rope inside the boat, he
climbed back in and started the engine. "You take care, Amos," he
said, gunning the engine and steering the boat back onto the lake.

Corbin's fears about Derrick getting more deeply involved in
matters where he didn't belong had been confirmed earlier that
morning when Corbin learned the sheriff's office was seeking a
warrant for entry into the old mine. Corbin was the one over-
seeing the legal end of things, but he had put it in Herb's court
to increase security at the mine and personally check things out
to be certain there was nothing there to be found. Corbin
wanted this done only as a precaution, as he was nearly certain
his lawyers could prevent the warrant from ever being issued.

Herb didn't mind this part of Corbin's orders. It was the
second part that bothered him. Corbin had instructed Herb to
make a trip to "the other property," where he was to dispose of
the evidence they had kept hidden there for several years. This
was a sore point with Herb, as he didn't want this evidence
disposed of. Corbin had hinted at doing it for years, but Herb
had always convinced him to put it off. But with Derrick
poking around, Corbin gave strict orders for Herb to get the job
done once and for all.

What was Herb to do? Frightened as he was to admit it, he
was contemplating an alternative action that could end up

exposing him to grave danger. But a man's morals could only bend so far, and Herb's had already bent further than his conscience would comfortably allow.

CHAPTER 8

Reggie smiled to herself as Derrick pulled his Corvette out of the parking lot and turned in the direction of Chandler law firm. She had an ace up her sleeve and wanted to make sure everything was just right before using it. She even went so far as giving in without objection when he wanted to take his car. Allowing him time to get into the flow of traffic, she set the stage for her pitch with a pointed suggestion. "You *do* know getting to see these records is going to be a hassle, don't you? Corbin is bound to have left instructions to have them filed under lock and key."

"I also know they're public records," Derrick reminded her. "Corbin can't keep them hidden forever."

"No, but he can make seeing them a drawn-out battle, one that might cost you several days floundering around in legal mire."

"What else can I do?" Derrick shrugged. "I want a look at those files."

Reggie grinned to herself, knowing she had Derrick right where she wanted him. "I could help, you know," she said sweetly. "My cousin Rebecca works for Chandler. One word from me, and all the records you want could be at your disposal. No mess, no hassle, no waiting."

"Great!" Derrick half shouted. "I knew there had to be some good reason we were set up as partners again. Your cousin, eh?"

"Now wait a minute, Mr. Beatty. I didn't say I *would* speak to Rebecca. I said I *could* speak to her."

Derrick eyed her suspiciously. "What are you getting at?"

"What I'm getting at is really quite simple," she responded with an insistent tone in her voice. "I want something in return for getting those files in your hands. I think that's only fair."

Derrick raised an eyebrow. "What exactly do you want?"

Reggie made him wait while she pulled down the sun visor on her side and used the mirror to touch up her lipstick. "Like I said, it's really quite simple," she coolly stated. "I want to hear what happened between you and Corbin."

"What?!" Derrick bellowed. "That's blackmail!"

"Yes, that's the right word. I already have it figured to be a girl. I just want the details."

"Regina! You're not being fair! You know perfectly well I don't want to talk about it."

"That's okay. You don't have to. Just like I don't have to talk with Rebecca."

Derrick took the next corner so hard Reggie thought the seat belt was going to rip her in half. "You have no heart!" he snapped.

"Not when it comes to my job." She grinned. "The way I see it, knowing what happened between you and Corbin could be an important factor in my aiding your investigation."

"It's pure blackmail, that's what it is!"

"Well, that too. I'm after some information, and I have a lever. Need I say more? You can start your story anytime. I'm listening. And take it easy with the driving. I don't have any cousins in places to fix a traffic ticket." It was a full minute before Derrick made a sound. Reggie just let him stew. She had him and she knew it. No use rushing things.

At last, Derrick cleared his throat. "Her name was Vivian Lane," he said disgustedly.

"I was right! It was a girl! You and Corbin both fell in love with her, didn't you?"

"This is hard enough for me, Regg. If you want to hear the story, let me tell it, okay? I met Vivian my freshman year of college. We hit it off and started dating on a regular basis."

"Was she beautiful?"

"Yes, Reggie, she was beautiful."

Reggie's next question was a tougher one, but she wanted to know badly enough to risk asking it. "Were you in love with her?"

There was another pause. "I suppose I was. I thought she might learn to care for me too, but it didn't work out."

Reggie didn't like hearing Derrick say he was in love with Vivian, but at least it hadn't worked out. "That's where Corbin comes in, right?" she pressed further.

Derrick shot an angry glance at Reggie. "Corbin met Vivian when I invited her to the house for dinner. The jerk liked what he saw, and the war was on. It wasn't the first time it happened, either. We had a long track record of stealing each other's dates. But this time it was someone I actually cared for. I have no idea what Vivian saw in the jerk, but whatever it was, it was obvious enough to read all over Vivian's face."

"That's it?" Reggie pressed, obviously disappointed. "Corbin took a girl away from you, and you've hated him ever since?"

"I don't hate my brother," Derrick remarked soberly. "There's a difference in being totally disgusted with the jerk and hating him. But there was more to it than just him taking Vivian away from me.

"You have to understand that my brother never was overly thrilled about church attendance. By the time the two of us started college, he was totally inactive. Vivian, on the other hand, had a strong testimony. She obviously liked Corbin, and she was nice enough to him, but she held him at arm's length. I made the mistake of laughing at him over it, which only fanned the fire. He came up with the story that Vivian was the only one who might reactivate him, and darn if she didn't fall for his line.

Why is it women are so naive when it comes to some jerk stringing them on, Regg?"

"Hey! Don't judge all women by what you see one do! I've never been naive about anything in my life. Especially a man!"

"Well, you're the exception then. My experience has been that most women will believe anything from a guy like Corbin when he turns on the charm."

"That's not true," Reggie snapped. "You're sounding like a chauvinist now."

"But it was true in Vivian's case. My sweet-talking brother had her eating out of his hand. By the time she realized he was lying about coming back to church, it was too late. She'd already fallen in love with the jerk—"

"She was in love with him?" Reggie interrupted. "How about Corbin? Was he in love with her?"

"I'm not sure Corbin knows what love is," Derrick grumbled. "But he must have felt something for Vivian." Derrick turned the Corvette into the parking lot of Chandler law firm and pulled into the first empty spot he found. "Does that satisfy your curiosity?" he asked, shutting down the engine. "Or do you plan on pushing me for the gruesome details?"

"What do you think?" She grinned.

"I think we should go inside and check on those files," he said, attempting to move away from the subject of Corbin.

Reggie wasn't falling for it. "I'll get the files in your hands only if you promise to complete the story when we're finished here. That's my final offer. Take it or leave it."

Derrick opened his door and stepped out. "You have me against the wall," he huffed before slamming the door closed.

Reggie opened her own door and got out. She knew he would have opened the door if she'd waited, and she had to admit it was tempting to let him. But she just didn't want to give him the pleasure. "So can I take that as a promise?" she persisted.

"Only if I get my hands on those files."

"You'll get the files, sweetheart," she said sarcastically. "I never renege on an agreement."

Inside the office, Reggie led the way straight to her cousin Rebecca's cubicle. They caught her on the phone, but when she spotted Derrick, her eyes widened. She motioned for them to sit down while she finished her call.

"Derrick Beatty!" Rebecca said excitedly as she shoved the phone back to the receiver. "I can't believe it's you! What are you doing in Arizona?"

Derrick smiled. "I've come home, Rebecca. And just to clear the air before you ask, no, it has nothing to do with your cousin here. Granted, we're working as partners again, but that's the extent of our—you know—our . . ."

"Relationship?" Rebecca said, finishing his sentence for him.

"No! Not relationship," Derrick quickly responded. "Just our dealings with each other."

"Don't worry, Derrick," Reggie laughed. "Rebecca is smart enough to know I'd never look at you as more than my partner. Which brings us to the point of our visit, cousin dear. I need a favor."

"Oh, boy," Rebecca moaned. "Anytime you start a visit with those words, I know I'm in trouble. What favor this time?"

"Derrick is—that is to say—Derrick and *I* are looking into the case of Samuel Beatty's disappearance. Since Chandler law firm handled Samuel's probate, I know you have copies of everything."

Rebecca's face went pale. "You don't know what you're asking, Regg. Those files are locked away tighter than the queen's diamonds."

"Are you saying you don't have access to them?"

Rebecca twisted her locket nervously between her fingers. "I didn't say that, Regg. All I'm saying is my neck goes on the block if I let you see them. And I'm talking 'goes on the block' *big-time.*"

"Rebecca, you know as well as I do something smells about that probate. We need to see those files."

"And we need copies," Derrick quickly added.

Rebecca retreated into her own thoughts for a few moments. "You're not asking much, are you?" she stated at last. "Okay, here's the deal. I can't have you looking over this stuff here in the office, and I darn sure can't have you making copies of it. But I can access the files on our computer system. I'll have to play it safe and do it after hours when all the bigwigs have gone. I have your e-mail address, Regg, so I'll send you an attachment containing the files, then delete all traces of what I've done on this end. Don't you dare ever let it get out you've seen those files! I mean it!"

"Fair enough, Rebecca. As soon as I download the files, we'll go the route of seeking a warrant for the originals. That'll give us an advanced look, and we can wait until we get a legal look at things to make any announcements."

"You know you're in for a fight to obtain a warrant for those files, don't you, Regg? I'm not lying when I say they're guarded by the state militia."

"We'll face the militia when it comes to that," Derrick said. "Thanks for your help, Rebecca. I owe you big-time."

"Your partner owes me several big ones, Derrick. One of these days I intend to collect on some of what she owes."

Derrick and Reggie stood. "You know I'm good for anything you ask, cousin," Reggie said smiling. "Unless it might be loaning you my new blue pantsuit."

"I'll settle for an invitation to your wedding," Rebecca teasingly replied. Then, with a wink at Derrick, she added, "I demand to be the first in line to kiss the groom."

Reggie's face turned red. Grabbing Derrick by the arm, she quickly shoved him out of the cubicle. Turning so only Rebecca could see, she stuck out her tongue, and Reggie and Derrick left the building.

* * *

Ed Quinn stood before Judge Garret, a questioning look on his face. "You don't understand, Judge," he argued. "I need this warrant. It has to do with a new lead in the five-year-old investigation of Samuel Beatty's disappearance."

Judge Garret brushed back her hair from one shoulder. "I understand your position, Sheriff. Believe me I do. And I wish I could grant you the warrant right now. Unfortunately, your new lead came about illegally." She pointed to the photographs in the sheriff's hand. "Derrick Beatty and Reggie Mandel were obviously in the old mine unlawfully. Corbin Beatty must have anticipated you'd be seeking a warrant, because his lawyer caught me an hour ago with this evidence. Unless you can show probable cause for needing access to the mine in some way other than on the word of these two, my hands are tied."

Quinn shoved the pictures angrily into his blazer pocket. "I don't know who I spend more time fighting in this town!" he fumed. "The crooks or the lawyers! Evidence of what happened to Samuel Beatty may be buried in the back of that mine, and so help me, Judge, I'm going to have a look at the place before Corbin Beatty has the chance to eradicate it. I'm stationing some men where they can spot any activity at that mine, and by thunder if one of Corbin's men or anyone else tries to go into the place, I'll have them arrested for something."

"I wholeheartedly agree with what you're doing, Sheriff," the judge responded. "But tread lightly, okay? You wouldn't want to do anything to compromise evidence that might be used later on in Samuel's case. And off the record, you're up against some of the best lawyers in the business."

"I'll keep that in mind, Judge," the sheriff said as he turned to walk out of her chambers.

* * *

Derrick started his car and pulled it from the lot. "So, what's next on your agenda?" Reggie asked.

Derrick blew out a loud breath. "I'm afraid I'm out of aces for now, Regg," he conceded. "I'd say we're pretty much stymied until we get our hands on those files or maybe learn something about Sheriff Quinn's effort at scoping out the mine. We might as well check in with Clint to see what else he has on his plate for us to be working on."

"We can do that. And on the way, you can keep your promise," she grinned.

"Ah, yes," he responded ruefully. "Back to Vivian and Corbin. Where did we leave off?"

"He was in love with her, she was in love with him, he refused to come back to the Church. So where does chapter two take us?"

"Chapter two, huh? Well, chapter two, as you put it, is where things take a downhill turn. Corbin cranked up the heat and started pushing for her to elope to Vegas with him."

Reggie's eyebrows raised. "Vivian didn't buy into that, did she?"

"Not at first. But Corbin wouldn't let up. He finally caught her in a weak moment."

"You're kidding me!" Reggie asked in shock. "She agreed to elope with him?"

"Like I said, it was in a weak moment. I personally don't believe she ever intended to go through with it. She just got caught up in the weaving of Corbin's romantic web. But she did get in the car, and they did start for Vegas. By the time they reached Kingman, she had come to her senses. She demanded that Corbin take her home."

"Uh-huh. I'll bet that went over well," Reggie noted.

"About like dropping an anvil in a basket of eggs. Corbin turned around and started home, but he was anything but a happy camper. After becoming inactive, he had started sampling a little Irish whiskey now and then, and on the trip home, he sampled more than a little. They later found enough in his blood stream to send an elephant into orbit. Vivian begged him to let her drive, but that was out of the question for Corbin."

Reggie had little trouble seeing where this was headed. "There was an accident, wasn't there?" she guessed.

"It was on Highway 93 just out of Wickenburg. Corbin missed a turn going in excess of eighty miles an hour. He ended up with scratches and a broken leg. Vivian didn't fare so well. The top of the car caved in on her side. The windshield shattered, and it shredded her face." Derrick shuddered at the memory. "I saw her three weeks later in the hospital. It wasn't a pretty sight, Regg. Corbin went crazy when Vivian's father got a restraining order to keep him away from her. Maybe you remember her father. He was a prominent lawyer here in Mesa at the time. Martin Lane."

Reggie shook her head. "No, I don't remember a Martin Lane, I'm afraid."

"He was in the same ward as my folks. I've always believed it was out of respect for my mother that he refused to bring charges against Corbin. He certainly had just cause, and he certainly could have won a conviction with little effort. Instead, he blocked all efforts for the attorney general's office to press charges."

Reggie considered this. Derrick might have been right about Martin's reason for not wanting things dragged into court out of respect for Evelana Beatty, but she wondered if it might not have also been because of his own daughter. Vivian was obviously facing a tremendous challenge with her injuries alone. A court battle would only have added to her problems. From Derrick's next statement, she concluded even more this must have been the case.

"As soon as Vivian was strong enough," Derrick explained, "Martin closed down his office and left Mesa, taking his whole family with him. None of us ever heard from them again." Derrick paused to sigh, then added, "Corbin should have counted his blessings for not going to prison over what he had done. Instead, he grew more bitter than ever. He blamed the Church for turning Vivian's mind against him. That's when he completely disassociated himself from anything—or anyone— connected to the Church, including his family. When he moved out, it broke our mother's heart. She died within a year, and I'll always believe Corbin killed her. The official cause of death was an aneurysm, but the way I see it, it was just a broken heart."

"Oh, Derrick. No wonder you don't like talking about it. I'm sorry for dredging it up, but I just had to know."

"Yeah, well, now that it's out, I'm glad you do know."

Reggie did feel bad about her tactics to draw such a tragic story out of Derrick, but she refused to believe the effort wasn't worth what she had learned. She felt compelled to say one final thing to Derrick. "You know what Doctrine and Covenants 64:10 says about forgiveness, don't you?"

"I know, Regg," he admitted. "The time will come when I have to forgive Corbin, but it's not going to be easy."

At that instant, Derrick's cell phone rang. Pulling it from his pocket, he handed it to Reggie. "Take this, will you? I hate talking on the phone while I'm driving."

More of his not standing too close to the edge, Reggie reasoned with a smile as she took the phone. "It's a call from Sheriff Quinn," she said, checking the ID. "Hopefully we're in for some good news."

Unfortunately, the call proved anything but good as they learned of Corbin's effort to legally block a search warrant for the mine.

CHAPTER 9

Herb Solomon unlocked the gate that blocked the entrance to the old mine. It had been five years since he was last here—the day of the explosion. He had left instructions for some men to station themselves here to secure the premises against any more intruders, but they hadn't arrived yet. It was just as well. Being alone would give him the chance to look things over well and take any necessary precautions without the worry of an audience. He fired up the Coleman lantern he had brought along and headed into the mine. Not wasting time, he headed straight to the point where the explosion had occurred. What memories this old hole in the ground brought back. Herb never actually worked the mine, but he did visit it on occasion just to be close to the source that was bringing in all that wonderful money. The $75,000 he had invested to get Samuel started in the beginning had repaid itself many times over before Samuel decided to pull out and close the mine down. That $75,000 had been hard to come by, and Herb had known the mine was a gamble, but he had always been a gambler at heart. As it worked out, his "gamble" in the mine was the best roll of the dice he ever tossed. If more of his ventures had turned out a fraction as well, Herb might have avoided a mountain of problems along the way.

Even the best of Herb's dealings with the mine were overshadowed by the memory of that final visit. The thunder of the explosion, the choking for breath, the excruciating pain—all these memories remained as a haunting testimony of that brutal event. It was one of those never-to-be-forgotten disasters that would leave both his mind and soul forever scarred. With gut-wrenching anticipation, Herb forced himself to take the last few steps leading to the actual point of the explosion. Once there, he drew in a calming breath, held the light as close as possible, and analyzed the sight before him. It was evident that Corbin's men had done a good job cleaning up the place. There were a few traces of powder burns and a speck of red paper here and there, which Herb knew came from the dynamite, but these would be impossible to completely eliminate. At least there didn't seem to be any sign of blood remaining. Not that someone using modern-day forensic techniques couldn't reveal where it had once been, but it was Corbin's plan to block all efforts in that direction. It was the same thing he had managed to do in the initial investigation. There really wasn't much Herb could do here that hadn't already been done.

Shining the light on the pile of rubble where the tunnel now ended, Herb remembered how he had been one of the last two people ever to go beyond this point. Samuel Beatty was the other. Again, the pain of the memory bore down on Herb, and suddenly he wanted out of the mine immediately. As he turned to leave, the reflection of a shiny object barely penetrating from under a large rock caught his eye. He moved in for a closer look. With a little effort, he was able to extract the object only to discover it was the twisted top to a Coleman lantern. Herb's blood turned cold as he realized this must have been part of the lantern he was carrying at the time of the explosion—something the cleanup crew had missed. One last quick look around was all Herb could stomach before starting out of the mine as hurriedly as concern for his safety would allow.

Once outside, he relocked the gate and headed for his car. Before reaching it, he was shocked to see a vehicle suddenly appear over the hill on the road leading to the mine. He caught his breath, realizing it was a squad car from the sheriff's department. Herb hardly had time to grasp this when a second and then a third squad car followed the first over the hill. He stood frozen as the cars, each containing two officers, pulled to a stop. An officer exited the nearest car and walked over to where Herb stood. "What are you boys doing here?" Herb abruptly asked. "This is private property."

"We're here on Sheriff Quinn's orders," the officer replied. "It seems we have a motorcycle gang who have expressed their intention to hold a gathering here at the entrance to the old mine. There's been no permit applied for or issued, and the sheriff is concerned. We're here to be sure things don't get out of hand in case these guys do show up."

Herb was wise enough to realize this story was nothing but a ploy, but what was he to do? This was something Corbin and his team of lawyers would need to handle. "Which brings up a point," the officer continued. "What's your business here at the mine? You're not associated with this motorcycle group, by chance?"

"No! I work for the mine's owner. I'm in charge of security for the facility."

The officer moved a step closer. "May I see some identification?" he asked.

Herb was more than a little annoyed at this request. This officer had no doubt that Herb worked for Corbin Beatty. He was just taking his little game to extremes. But Herb knew his best course was to play along. He removed his wallet and handed his driver's license to the officer, who looked it over closely. Then, catching Herb off guard, the officer pointed to the piece of Coleman lantern still in Herb's hand. "What's that you're holding, Mr. Solomon?"

Herb felt his heart speed. "This?" he asked, holding up the piece of bent metal. "Oh, it's nothing. Just some trash I picked up back there."

"Do you mind if I look at it?" the officer pressed. Reluctantly, Herb handed it over. The officer examined it a moment, then stepped toward his squad car. "Wait right here, Mr. Solomon, while I run a check on your ID. I'll get right back with you."

Herb could only watch helplessly as the officer walked away with the piece of lantern. How could he get it back without calling attention to the fact that it was more than mere trash? He looked on as the officer used his radio for a brief communication with his headquarters. After this was out of the way, the officer returned and handed back Herb's license. "Thank you, Mr. Solomon," he said. "Everything checks out." Just as Herb feared, the officer didn't return the piece of lantern.

"So, are you finished here, or do you intend to hang around some more?" Herb asked, knowing full well the answer long before it was given.

"We'll be hanging around awhile," the officer responded. "Reports say that this motorcycle gang is rather large and unruly. We have no indication when they plan to be here for sure. Our source only tells us they're on their way."

Herb wet his lips. "Yes, right, motorcycle gang. Listen, Officer, as head of security for the mine, I've had reports of some trouble myself. It seems we've had a break-in, which I think you can understand the seriousness of. I have some men of my own on their way to the mine. I've given them orders to keep a close watch on the place."

The officer smiled. "I suppose we can all keep each other company, then. Maybe we can scrounge up a deck of cards and get us a game going."

"You do realize you and your men aren't permitted inside the premises of the mine, don't you, Officer?"

"I'm aware of the legalities involved with our being here," the officer assured. "If, as you say, you've had problems with someone breaking into the mine, I'd assume you would appreciate our help, Mr. Solomon."

Herb knew his options were limited. These officers had their orders, and there was no way they were going to back away. What Herb needed to do right now was to contact Corbin. He could do that using his cell phone inside his car, where those on the outside couldn't hear the conversation. He didn't want to leave until his own men arrived to keep watch on things, yet he knew it might be another hour before they got here. "If you have no objection, Officer," he proposed, "I'll just wait in my car till my men get here."

"I certainly have no problem with that, Mr. Solomon," the officer affirmed.

"Good. Then I'll just go to my car now." Herb made sure he showed no anxiousness in his step as he walked to the car and got inside. He knew he was being watched as he made the call, but these officers were as aware that Herb was playing games as Herb was aware they were. So, he figured, what did it matter?

"Corbin?" Herb said as soon as an answer came. "We have a bit of a situation here at the mine."

* * *

Corbin felt his stomach tighten at Herb's revelation. He grabbed a towel and wiped his face, as he had taken the call while soaking in the hot tub in his penthouse. "What situation?" he snapped.

"We have cops here at the mine," Herb nervously reported. "Six of 'em. From the sheriff's department."

"Cops?" Corbin echoed worriedly. "What are they doing there?"

"My guess is your brother has something to do with it. They gave me a cock-and-bull story about protecting the place from some motorcycle gang."

"That makes sense," Corbin agreed. "My informants told me Sheriff Quinn applied for a warrant to the mine earlier this morning. Fortunately, my lawyers put the kibosh on it for now. The problem is, time is against us. They're bound to find some way to drum up a warrant sooner or later. Did you get a chance to look things over down there before they showed up?"

"Yeah. It looks pretty clean. And I have four of our guys on the way. I won't leave till they get here."

"That's right. You stay put. And get some more men up there! I don't like the odds of six of them to four of us."

"Consider it done."

Corbin covered his eyes in thought. "Okay," he went on to say. "As soon as you can pull away, I want you on the other item of business we spoke about. I want that evidence done away with as soon as possible. You got that, Herb?"

There was a long pause before Herb responded, which only heightened Corbin's already-growing concern that Herb might not be fully ready to comply with this order. The nervousness in Herb's voice when he did speak only added more proof. "The evidence we have stored at the 'other property,' you mean?" Herb questioned.

The fact that the man was stalling with this all-too-unnecessary question was obvious. "You know exactly what I mean, Herb! Don't go getting sentimental on me. I want everything dismantled. I want the pieces packed in cemented barrels, and I want the barrels dumped in the Pacific Ocean! I need you in charge of this since you're the only one other than me and Doc Pepperton who knows the whole story. You can handle it, can't you?"

Corbin switched off his phone and remained in thought for several seconds. There was little doubt about it—Herb couldn't be trusted this time. Corbin felt forced to pull someone else in to do the job, but who? It had to be someone he could trust to keep their mouth shut. The name that came to his mind almost immediately was Ramsey Borden. Ramsey was a headstrong man whom Corbin didn't like much. But when there was a dirty job to be done that no one else wanted, Ramsey never hesitated to step up and do it. The problem was he wasn't one to follow orders if he thought his way was better, and he tended to lean toward the overkill. Ramsey would keep his mouth closed, though, as long as he was paid well enough. If Corbin did decide to use Ramsey for this job, it would mean putting the job on hold for a time—a thought Corbin didn't like. Ramsey was away on some personal business that could possibly drag out a whole week.

Corbin tossed the phone aside and climbed out of the hot tub. Wrapping a towel around himself, he walked to the sliding glass doors and stepped through them to the outside patio. The view from here overlooked the bulk of the resort with the lake in the background. It was a spectacular sight, and Corbin almost felt like a king overlooking his domain—a domain that had to be protected at any cost.

Corbin wasn't exactly sure when Ramsey would be back. He hoped it would be maybe tomorrow, maybe the day after. As worried as he was about getting rid of the evidence, and with Herb showing definite signs of weakness, Corbin reasoned his only choice was to go with Ramsey. He'd just have to wait for the man's return.

CHAPTER 10

Two days. Derrick couldn't believe that was how long it had been since he had returned to his old job. They had been two busy days, that much was for sure. And it would be a lie stretched to its limit for Derrick to say they had been anything but pleasant. Getting reacquainted with his beautiful partner may have been a frightening thought as he walked into this new chapter of his life, but it was proving to be more than pleasant. It was downright fantastic. The problem was, he was afraid he was accomplishing little more than setting himself up for an even harder fall than the one he'd experienced when they'd said good-bye four years ago. What he did know was that working with her again was great and, for the moment at least, well worth the risk.

After spending most of the day on a special assignment for Clint, Reggie and Derrick made it back to the office just as the sun was setting. Reggie fired up her computer to see if Rebecca's attachment had made it yet. It hadn't, so they each settled in for the wait at their own desks. Derrick couldn't keep his eyes off Reggie, who sat staring at her computer screen. How did she manage to look so fresh and vibrant after a tough day like they had just had? She was really something. In his imagination, Derrick crossed the room to Reggie's side, where she stood to greet him with a smile so warm it could melt an arctic ice shelf. He closed his eyes and let the fantasy continue. His fantasy was so real he could almost feel her warm, moist lips against his as he pulled her into his arms. A sudden knock at the door yanked him abruptly back to reality.

"Must be our pizza," he heard Reggie say. "Are you going to get it?"

"Yeah," he remarked, slipping out of his chair and heading for the door.

"That'll be thirteen seventy-five," the delivery man said.

Derrick pulled out a twenty and traded it with the man for the pizza. Walking over to Reggie's desk, he set it down on the spot she had cleared. Sharing a sausage-pepperoni pizza with her wasn't as nice as his fantasy had been, but it would do—especially with the appetite he had worked up since breakfast. Anyway, how could he ever suppose a woman like Reggie would give him a serious second look? Not that he'd actually pursue her even if she did suggest an interest. To Derrick, getting serious with a woman meant only one thing: marriage and an eternal commitment. Granted, he was in his early thirties, and so was she, but still—he wasn't sure it was time for such a commitment just yet. Fantasizing a kiss was okay, just as long as it remained a fantasy.

"Bingo!" Reggie suddenly cried, dropping her slice of pizza on her napkin and using her mouse to bring up the e-mail just appearing on her computer screen. "It's from Rebecca!"

Derrick's eyes shot to the screen. "What do we have?" he asked.

"We have an attachment. Let me get it open." A double click on her mouse was all it took. "We're in business, Derrick! There's a seven-page document here!" By the time she hit the print key, Derrick was at the printer waiting for the first page.

The next twenty minutes found them demolishing a pizza and scrutinizing the document one page at a time. The first five pages proved to be a copy of the uncontested will Corbin had pawned off as authentic. "I always wondered why Corbin didn't try to take Dad's old house from me," Derrick remarked. "In all his generosity, he's actually put a clause in the will granting me ownership of it. How about that. At least he didn't leave me completely out in the cold."

This caught Reggie's interest. "It sounds like you're pretty sure Corbin is the real author behind the will—not your dad."

"Oh, yeah, this thing's a fake from the opening paragraph. One thing blatantly missing is an old Navy N3N-3 trainer. Dad would never have left the biplane out of his will. Something else that's missing are the three paintings still hanging in the old house. These are holes that wouldn't be there if the document was authentic. And there is one other small item. This signature at the bottom doesn't belong to Dad."

"What?" Reggie said, moving in for a closer look. "Are you sure?"

"Spotting problems of this sort is a big part of my occupation, Regg. Add this to the fact that I know what Dad's signature looks like, and it comes up as forgery. Not even a good forgery. If Corbin thought this signature was real, he had to have been blind."

Reggie considered this. "Corbin must believe the signature is real," she surmised.

"My thoughts exactly, Regg. And if he believes it is real, that means he had to know Dad was alive when the document was signed. I'm thinking he rationalized that he'd found a way to coerce Dad into signing the will, only Dad somehow outsmarted him."

"Without Corbin even knowing he had been outsmarted?" Reggie guessed.

"That's the way I see it. One thing I know for sure: this document will never stand up through a second court hearing. Corbin doesn't know it yet, but he's treading in deep water." Derrick glanced at the remaining two pages of the document. "I wonder what else we can find here," he mused.

"From what I see, the last two pages are full of lawyer mish-mash that has to do with Chandler law firm's handling of the will," Reggie inserted. "I think we're going to need some help from our own legal department on this part."

"You're probably right, Regg," Derrick remarked, looking the pages over for himself. "And with tomorrow being Saturday, we're probably out of luck catching any of the legal gang before next week."

"You're right," Reggie agreed. "But I'd say we're onto something here that will guarantee that warrant for the mine. You want to call Quinn, or do you want me to handle it?"

CHAPTER 11

As far as Reggie was concerned, Saturday mornings were made for sleeping in. But this particular Saturday morning found her wide awake even before the rooster crowed. There was no use trying to lie to herself as to why she couldn't sleep. It was because of Derrick Beatty. That darn man just affected her this way! If thoughts of him weren't depriving her of sleep, then he could be found traipsing around all over her dreams. She knew perfectly well he would never lose sleep over her or invite her into one of *his* dreams. It just wasn't fair! If she had to fall in love with someone, why couldn't it have been someone other than Derrick Beatty? Why did he have to come barging back into her life after she had resigned herself to never seeing him again?

With her shower and morning makeup ritual out of the way, she fixed herself a couple of scrambled eggs and some toast. She ate this while working her way through the *Arizona Republic*, another one of her morning rituals. She always started with the front section and worked back. This morning it was the last page of the *Local* section that caught her eye. More particularly, it was the political cartoon directed at Sheriff Ed Quinn. The local cartoonist was known for having his favorite targets, and Ed Quinn was high on his list. The cartoonist always drew Quinn with oversized ears, a crooked nose, and eyebrows that looked like hedges. This one depicted Quinn dreaming of himself sitting on a throne labeled *Arizona Governor,* wearing a crown labeled

Ten-year-old's mentality, and holding a scepter labeled *Quinn's might makes right!* She did a double take. Was the cartoonist hinting that Quinn might be running for state governor? If so, it was news to Reggie. In thinking about it, she believed Quinn would make a great governor, but giving up his office as sheriff would leave a huge hole in the local law enforcement.

Reggie tossed the paper aside and found her thoughts returning again to Derrick. No one could deny the two of them made a great investigative team after what they'd accomplished on Samuel Beatty's case in just two short days. This was after most others had given up on the case. And while they may not have known exactly where Samuel was right then, they were positive he was alive at the time the will was drawn up. And they were also positive the will was a fake. In less than half a week, they had managed to put Corbin Beatty behind a giant eight-ball without his even knowing it. Yep, she and Derrick made a fantastic team. She sighed, finding herself wishing again they could take their relationship to a level above just being partners in a fight against crime. But it was all foolishness, as she'd already concluded this was impossible.

Reggie cleaned up her dishes and was just wiping her hands on a dish towel when the phone rang. She checked the caller ID to see it was an unknown name. "This better not be a telemarketer," she grumbled, reaching for the receiver. She waited long enough to be sure it wasn't a recording before answering. "Hello?"

"Regina Mandel?" The question came from a strong but unfamiliar male voice.

"Yes, I'm Regina Mandel," she answered cautiously.

"And you are the private detective who works with Derrick Beatty? Is that correct?"

This was obviously no telemarketer, but who would begin a conversation by wanting to know if she was Derrick's partner? Well, she figured, if this mysterious caller could ask questions, so could she. "Who is this?" she pressed.

There was a lengthy pause followed by a declaration that set Reggie's mind whirling. "My name is Corbin Beatty."

Reggie caught her breath. "Corbin Beatty—as in the owner of Beatty Enterprises?" she asked.

"Yes. But I think you might know me better as your partner's brother."

Reggie's mind raced to make sense of this call. She reasoned it had to have something to do with Derrick's ongoing investigation into his father—into *their* father's disappearance. But exactly what she had no idea. "I heard Derrick mention a brother once or twice," Reggie responded, doing a little baiting of her own. "May I ask your reason for calling?"

"I'll get right to the point, Miss Mandel. My security department observed you and my brother snooping around our father's old mine. Since Derrick and I aren't exactly on the best of speaking terms, I thought it more expedient to approach you. The mine is private property, and we do keep it sealed off for good reason. May I ask why you took it upon yourselves to breach our security and enter the mine?"

Now the call made sense. It was only natural that Corbin would want some answers about her and Derrick being in the mine. But it was just as natural for her to keep her lips sealed— at least for the time being. Reggie was aware of what the Book of Mormon taught about lying, but in her occupation, there were times when the whole truth could jeopardize a delicate situation. Like now. "You can put your mind at ease on the matter," she told him. "We simply flew up to the mountains for a day's getaway from the pressures of our job. As long as we were there, I asked Derrick to show me the mine. That's it, plain and simple."

"I see," Corbin replied. "And you just naturally have no idea why Sheriff Ed Quinn is seeking a warrant for entrance into the mine? Or why he has a small army of men camped out at the place?"

"I haven't the slightest idea. Maybe it has something to do with his bid to enter the governor's race. You know, ecology . . . that sort of thing."

Reggie heard Corbin release a heavy sigh. "Listen, Miss Mandel," he continued, "I'd really like the opportunity to sit down and discuss some things with you. Is there a chance I might talk you into driving up to the resort for an early dinner? You can even plan on spending the night if you like. On my tab, naturally."

Reggie had to think fast. Corbin must have been nervous about things if he was willing to go this far to learn what she and Derrick were up to. She had no intention of telling him any more than she had already, but on the other hand, who knew what she might learn from Corbin's proposed meeting? She glanced at her watch. It was now 9:30 A.M. She figured the drive to the resort, which was located not far from Snowflake, would take about four hours. If she started at 10:00, that would put her there around 2:00 P.M. "What exactly is it you want to talk with me about?" she asked, playing him like she might play a kitten with a piece of twine.

"We both know there's more to the story of your trip to the mine than a picnic in the mountains, Miss Mandel. I'd just like the chance to sit down and discuss some things as two level-headed people doing their best to ward off a possible court battle, which would have no winners other than a few fat lawyers. Do you have any objections to simply coming up to discuss a few things?"

"I have no objection to simply talking. I can be at the resort somewhere around 2:00 P.M. if that's all right."

"Two o'clock will be perfect. Bring a friend if you like—just as long as your friend isn't my brother."

She laughed softly. "I'll be coming alone, Mr. Beatty."

"Good. I'll instruct the front desk to be expecting you. By the way, how does lobster sound? I assure you we have the finest chefs in the world at our resort, and I defy you to find better lobster anywhere this side of Cape Cod."

* * *

Derrick was just finishing up putting the things away from his trip to the store when he heard the doorbell. "Just a minute!" he called out. "I'll be right there!" Shoving the bottle of Clorox onto a shelf above the washing machine, he headed for the front door. To his surprise, it was a man in tattered and soiled clothing who looked as though he hadn't shaved in days. The smell of cheap wine on his breath was overpowering. The man was holding a brown manila envelope, which he indicated he wanted Derrick to take from him. Glancing past the man, Derrick noticed a taxi waiting out front. "May I help you?" Derrick asked.

The man burped. "Excuse me," he said, covering his mouth with a closed fist. Then, with a slurred voice, he explained, "I, uh, was paid to bring you this." The fellow held out the envelope. "And I was told to pass along a message. This here stuff is about your daddy."

Derrick instantly shoved the screen door open and took the envelope from the man. "Who put you up to this?" he asked.

The man backed away a step and shrugged. "Dunno. Never saw the guy before. Now if you'll excuse me, I gotta go."

Derrick glanced at the cab driver. "I don't know nothin' neither!" he called out. "The drunk slipped me a twenty and a note with your address on it."

Derrick nodded to the driver, who waited only long enough for the vagabond to get back inside before driving away. Derrick then opened the envelope expecting to find a note or something with an explanation on it. To his amazement, all it contained was a map of Arizona. Unfolding the map, he found that three sections on it had been circled with a yellow marker. Two of the locations he recognized immediately. One, on the Mogollon Rim, was the location of his father's old mine, and another near Snowflake was the location of The Majestic Saguaro Resort. But the third circled area, a point northeast of the resort, was one Derrick didn't recognize at all. The words *the other property* had been scribbled next to this on the map. "The other property?" Derrick muttered to himself. "What property?"

The vagabond had indicated this had something to do with Derrick's father. But who could it have come from? After having seen the forged will, Derrick was positive Corbin knew more about their father's fate than he was telling, but why would Corbin go to the trouble to get this map into Derrick's hands? Derrick reasoned that the only motivation Corbin might have would be if the location shown on the map was some sort of diversion. Still, if this wasn't Corbin's doing, then whose was it? Whoever it was knew Derrick well enough to realize he'd have to check this out—diversion or no diversion.

Reentering the house, Derrick moved to the phone and gave Clint Banister a call at home. He was glad when he got the real Clint instead of an answering machine. "Morning, Derrick. What's on your mind?"

Derrick quickly explained about the map and how a drunk had delivered it with the message that it concerned his father. "You know I have to check this out, Clint," he firmly added.

"You want to use the Cessna?" Clint guessed.

"Yeah. Is it available?"

"It will be later this afternoon. They found a questionable alternator in a routine maintenance check this morning. They called, and I told them to go ahead and change it out. They should be getting pretty close to being done by now. It sounds to me like you may be stirring up some unexpected interest in your investigation."

"Could be. I have an up-to-the-minute report on my computer. You know my password if you want to look at it."

"Not on a Saturday, pal. I'm taking my grandson to a ball game in about an hour. We'll be pigging out on hot dogs and orange soda. I've got a couple of extra tickets if you want to grab Regg and come along."

"Nice try, Clint, but no brass ring. If you'll clear me to use the Cessna, I'll leave you and your grandson to enjoy your time together."

"That's what I figured," Clint laughed. "But let's not take any unnecessary chances, okay? I know better than to tell you to wait until you have someone with you to check this out, but I am asking one thing. I keep a couple of tracking devices in the Cessna. They're in a box strapped under the front passenger's seat. Just in case you do land and get out of the plane, I want you to stick one of the devices in your pocket, okay? And keep it turned on, just in case."

"Good idea, Clint. I'll do that. Eat a hot dog for me and tell Randy Johnson I said hello just in case you run into him."

* * *

The drive to the resort went smoother than Reggie had thought it might. As a result, she arrived nearly half an hour early. She decided to use the time to look the place over. She caught the trolley car at the edge of the parking lot and rode it to the lakeside village where a variety of shops and restaurants lined both sides of a quaint cobblestone street. The street eventually turned into a rustic little pier extending a short way out over the lake. All in all, this was a very romantic setting, and she couldn't help but wish, in spite of herself, that Derrick was here to enjoy it with her. This thought brought a smile. Not only was Derrick not with her, but he didn't even realize she was here. Knowing the bad blood between him and Corbin, Derrick would probably have done his best to talk her out of coming if he had known.

There wasn't enough time for any serious browsing, so she had to settle for window shopping. She was almost disappointed when a glance at her watch told her it was time to check at the hotel lobby. Just as Corbin had said, the young woman at the lobby desk was expecting her. "Mr. Beatty has arranged for a private dinner," the young woman explained. "I'll have someone show you to the suite now."

"A private dinner?" Reggie questioned. "I assumed we'd be meeting in your hotel restaurant."

The young woman smiled. "Mr. Beatty felt you'd need more privacy for your business conversation. I assure you, Miss Mandel, you'll be pleased with your dinner setting."

Reggie wasn't so sure. She felt a bit edgy about dining with Corbin in one of the suites, but she figured she was a big enough girl to take care of herself. She also wasn't stupid enough to drive to the resort without telling someone her plans, so she had called Clint before she left. Clint wasn't overly happy about her meeting with Corbin alone, and he didn't like the idea of her doing it without Derrick knowing. It took a little sweet-talking, but eventually she was able to win him over. He did have a couple of demands. She had to promise she'd call his cell phone no later than 6:00 P.M. to let him know she was okay. And she was to carry one of those stupid tracking devices he was so fond of in her purse.

The bellhop stepped up to the desk. "This is Miss Mandel," the young woman told him. "If you'll show her to suite 714, I'll inform Mr. Beatty she's here."

"This way, Miss," the young man said, motioning toward the elevator. Reggie was amused by his deadpan expression. At least the hostess had smiled.

As the number 714 implied, the suite was located on the top floor. One glimpse at it took her breath away. The main room alone was larger than her whole apartment. It was carpeted with a luxurious, plush white carpet and decorated in Polynesian decor with a lava stone fireplace, a three-tiered, fountain-fed jacuzzi, two rattan chairs, and a matching sofa. A sliding glass door filled the entire back wall, which she noticed had a magnificent view of the lake. She observed that the dining table had been prepared on the outside balcony just beyond the sliding door.

"Please make yourself comfortable, Miss Mandel," the bellhop said. "Mr. Beatty will be here momentarily."

Reggie opened her purse with the intention of tipping the young man. "No, no," he quickly said. "It's one of the rules here at the resort: no tipping."

Reggie remembered reading about the "no tipping" policy that Samuel Beatty himself had instituted before his disappearance. Samuel had promised to pay those working for him well enough to make up for what they might lose in tips. It was Samuel's belief that tipping had a way of distracting from the atmosphere he wanted presented at his resort.

The bellhop stepped outside the room, leaving Reggie alone to look the place over more closely. Crossing to the sliding door, she stepped through it onto the balcony. The view from here was spectacular. A pleasant breeze brushed past her face, at the same time ruffling her short black hair. She took a deep breath of the fresh desert air and stepped to the edge of the balcony, where she leaned against the railing. Out on the lake, an open paddle-wheel boat moved slowly on a path hugging the shoreline. Several guests lined its deck as they enjoyed a lakeside tour of the facilities.

Reggie didn't even notice Corbin until she heard him clear his throat, drawing attention to him from behind. She turned quickly to see him standing in the doorway between the suite and the balcony. One look revealed him to be a man bearing enough resemblance to Derrick to leave little doubt the two were brothers. In spite of the resemblance, there were things about Corbin that instantly drew him apart from Derrick. For one thing, his clothing. From his Ray-Bans down to his Italian loafers, he looked like he had stepped off the pages of *Esquire* magazine. But the most obvious difference was a look in his eyes that Reggie had never seen in Derrick's. It was a certain coldness. Not the same coldness as was in the eyes of so many streetwise criminals Reggie had crossed paths with. This coldness was almost sad. It left a feeling of emptiness behind his expression. Reggie wasn't sure what she had expected, but it certainly didn't match what she saw now.

"I hope you find the resort to your liking, Miss Mandel," Corbin remarked with a managed smile. "It really is quite fabulous."

"Yes, it is," she quickly agreed. "A monumental tribute to the man who built it, I'd say." This was no slip of the tongue. Reggie made the remark knowing full well the extent of its implications. If it bothered Corbin at all, he did a good job of covering it up.

"I trust you had a pleasant trip," he remarked. "It does seem like a nice day for a drive."

"Very nice day, Mr. Beatty," she concurred.

Corbin stepped through the door and moved to where Reggie stood. "What do you say we dispense with the formalities?" he frankly suggested. "Corbin and Regina would seem much more comfortable."

"You have a point," she smilingly agreed. "More comfortable and a lot less stuffy. And while we're dispensing with things, how about we include the small talk? I'm here at your invitation to talk about more serious things. We might as well get right to the point."

This brought a laugh from Corbin. "A no-nonsense approach, huh? Something that goes with your occupation, I'm guessing. And one I have no argument with." Corbin moved to the table, where he pulled out a chair for Reggie. "Shall we?" he asked.

Reggie allowed him to help with her chair and watched as he rounded the table to take his own. It was only after Reggie was seated that she noticed the waiter pushing a food cart in their direction. Within seconds, he had served their meal. "As I said over the phone," Corbin explained. "Steamed lobster."

Reggie hadn't eaten since breakfast, and the lobster did smell tantalizing. "From the looks of this, I'd say you weren't exaggerating when you bragged about your chefs."

"Not one inch," he assured while pulling a wine bottle from the ice bucket left by the server. Popping the cork, he reached for her goblet.

"No, thank you," she said, pulling back the goblet. "I'll just stick with water."

She noticed the slightest hint of a frown cross Corbin's face. "You're a Mormon?" he surmised, unable to completely hide the sarcasm from his voice.

"Actually I'm a member of The Church of Jesus Christ of Latter-day Saints, but I suspect you prefer the more common term."

"I should have known with you being Derrick's partner and all. I can send for a soft drink if you like."

"No, really, water's fine." Reggie poured herself a glass from the iced pitcher the server had left.

Corbin filled his goblet from the bottle of wine, which he then placed back in the ice bucket. Using his fork, he dipped a small piece of lobster in the drawn butter and placed it in his mouth. "It's a long drive back to Mesa," he said. "You're more than welcome to this suite for the night if you like."

"That's kind of you, Corbin, but I have a Primary class to teach in the morning."

This brought another laugh. "I hope you'll pardon me," he observed. "But I have trouble picturing you as a Primary teacher. I have no trouble at all picturing you as a private detective, but imagining you in front of those little terrors is stretching it some."

"Little terrors?" Reggie asked, one eyebrow raised.

He shrugged. "I was raised a Mormon—in case you hadn't heard. I think *little terrors* adequately describes what I remember my Primary classes being like."

Reggie took a bite of her lobster, then pursued the comment. "Are you saying you had a negative experience in your Primary class?"

Corbin stiffened noticeably. "I really don't care to discuss my association with the Mormons any further," he curtly stated. "That was another lifetime."

"All right," Reggie conceded. "What exactly is it you invited me here to discuss? I assume it has something to do with the mystery of your father's disappearance."

Corbin lowered his fork and stared at Reggie. "What makes you think I know any more about my father's disappearance than anyone else knows?"

Reggie knew she was faced with a decision about this time. On the one hand, she could be nice and play out the game by Corbin's rules. This brought a silent laugh to herself. She knew perfectly well she had every intention of rearranging the rules to fit her own needs. "What makes you think I *wouldn't* suspect you know more about your father's disappearance than you let on?" she countered. "After all, you gained the most from your father's disappearance. In fact you inherited everything."

Corbin's frown deepened. "I suppose you have the right to believe what you will," he rebutted, "but the fact is I have legal backing for everything I inherited from my father. Which brings us back to the question you so deftly sidestepped during our phone conversation this morning. What were you and my brother doing inside the old mine?"

Reggie took time for another bite of lobster before answering. She had gone for a nerve, and she had struck one dead center. She was in a much stronger position than Corbin since she knew that the will he was banking on was a fake. "Actually," she casually said following her deliberate hesitation,

"Derrick was showing me the mine as a possible investment venture. I figured if it was interesting enough, I might approach you about buying it for a future tourist attraction."

Corbin rolled his eyes. "You obviously have a very keen sense of humor, Regina. But let's take a more realistic look at why you and Derrick were at the mine, shall we? Derrick has always felt cheated because Dad left everything to me. He's looking for a way to get his foot in the door for a piece of the pie. Your attempt at a joke does nothing to change that fact."

"Now that's really a strange thing for you to say, Corbin. After all, you have a perfectly legal will, all signed by your father and everything, that declares you the sole owner of Beatty Enterprises. What possible worry could you have about Derrick wanting 'a piece of the pie'?"

Just then, Corbin's phone rang. He removed it from his pocket and checked the ID. "It's a business call," he said, glancing back at her. "Will you excuse me for a couple of minutes?"

Corbin rose from his chair and stepped out of the room, where he could take the call in private. This presented an unexpected break Reggie hadn't planned on, but one she wasn't going to pass up. She had noticed that even though they weren't served salad, the server had provided each of them with an extra fork. Picking up the extra fork from her side, she moved around to Corbin's side and traded hers for the fork Corbin had used for his lobster. She dropped his fork in a plastic bag usually used for holding her lipstick and placed it in the side pocket of her purse. She had just made it back to her chair when Corbin returned. "Sorry," he said. "Running an organization like Beatty Enterprises means you never know when an important call will come." He sat back down. "Now, where were we?"

"We were talking about the will that deeded Beatty Enterprises to you in the first place. You know, the one that strangely left your brother out in the cold."

"Hey, what can I say? If Dad wanted me to have it all, who was I to complain?"

"Nice use of the word *if*. But I personally doubt your father wanted you to have it all. You know what else I think? I think you have something to hide at the old mine. Something you're afraid might be discovered if those gates are ever opened to the scrutinizing eyes of Sheriff Quinn and company."

This brought an explosive reaction from Corbin, who slammed an angry fist against the table so hard it spilt half the wine from his glass. "There's nothing in that mine or anywhere else that I need to hide! The issue here is my brother trying to get his fingers on my pie and nothing more! He can't do that, Regina! I hold all the aces. But I'm open to anything that might bring this whole thing to a close without any unnecessary negative publicity. The way I see it, you're close enough to Derrick to convince him to abandon this crusade. I can make it worth your while if you're willing to cooperate with me."

"That's why you invited me here?" Reggie pressed. "You think you can buy me?"

Corbin's voice lowered in volume but remained staunch. "I'm not talking small-time incentives here, Regina. I'm talking in the neighborhood of a million. And all I'm asking is that you keep my brother's eyes from seeing anything that might encourage him to pursue a cause he's going to lose anyway."

Reggie stood and pushed back her chair. "I just lost my appetite!" she exclaimed. "If you'll excuse me, I think it's time I got back to Mesa." She started for the sliding door.

Corbin shot to his feet. "You're not going to walk out on me. No one walks out on Corbin Beatty!"

This brought Reggie to a sudden stop. "There's a first time for everything, Corbin. Just keep your eye on me, and you'll see what I mean. And by the way, I'm going to find out exactly what happened to your father. If you've harmed him in any way, all the money in the world won't keep me from bringing down the sword of justice on your head. Up until now, Derrick might have been your biggest worry, but thanks to our little talk, I'm the one in that chair now." Having said this, she turned and stormed out of the room.

It took less than five minutes to reach her car, which she had left parked in the visitors' lot. When she did reach it, she realized five minutes was all Corbin had needed to vent his anger against her. All four of her tires had been flattened, and every piece of glass in the car was shattered. It appeared all the damage had come from gunshots. In disgust, she pulled out her phone and called Clint. "I have a problem," she said once he answered. "It seems I rubbed our Mr. Corbin the wrong way." She painstakingly explained everything that had happened, then added, "I doubt I can even get a taxi out of here now. I'm sure our little tin god has seen to that."

Clint's response surprised Reggie. "We may be in luck, Regg. Derrick signed out the Cessna earlier today. He wanted to look at something not far from where you are right now." Clint went on to tell about the map Derrick had come by and suggested Reggie give him a call on his cell phone. "If you can't get through, call me back and we'll take it from there," he instructed.

A fury of emotions erupted in Reggie's mind. If the Cessna were this near, it would be fantastic. But thoughts of Derrick coming here to rescue her weren't all that warm and cuddly. What would he think of her ending up in a fix like this? She sighed, knowing there was no choice. "I'll give Derrick a call, Clint. In the meantime, can you get someone to tow my car home?"

"I'll do better than that. I'll report the shooting to Sheriff Quinn and have him check it out. Why not put some pressure on our friend?"

"I like the way you think, Clint. If I don't get back to you, you'll know I reached Derrick and he's on the way."

* * *

Derrick made a second pass over the facilities he had found at the location indicated on the map. He didn't quite know what to make of it all. A single dirt road leading off from Highway 180 led to the place, which was completely out of sight from the main road. There were two buildings encircled by a row of high, chain-link fencing. This was obviously a high-security area. There were no vehicles in sight, but that didn't mean one or more couldn't be hidden inside the larger building. There was also a landing strip. Derrick was considering setting the Cessna down for a closer look when he was interrupted by the sound of his cell phone. He glanced at the ID, then answered. "Yes, Regg? How's your day going? Getting lots of catching up done on your much-needed sleep?"

"Yeah, right. What are you doing on the job? I thought you had personal plans for the day?"

"Who says I'm on the job?" he asked. "You haven't by chance been talking to Clint?"

"I have, and he tells me you're flying somewhere over the western part of the state looking for mysterious things someone pointed out on a map."

"You heard right. I've found something pretty intriguing. I was just about to set down for a closer look when you inter-rupted me."

"Well, pardon me for that, but I do have my reasons for calling. I need a ride home."

Derrick pulled the phone away and stared at it. "A ride home from where?" he asked.

"Would you believe The Majestic Saguaro Resort?"

"What? You're joking!"

"I've never been more serious in my life. I just came from a meeting with one of the most obnoxious men I've ever encoun-tered, and now I find my Firebird all shot up to the point I can't drive it home."

Derrick's mind raced in confusion. "Are you saying you talked with Corbin?" he loudly guessed, hoping against hope to hear her say no.

"He invited me out for a lobster dinner. How could I refuse something that tempting?"

"What are you talking about, Regina?"

"Just fly over here and pick me up. I'll explain everything when I'm out of here."

Derrick put the plane into a banking turn, bringing it on a heading for the resort. "Do you know where the airstrip is?" he asked.

"You showed it to me from the air, remember?"

"I can be there in fifteen minutes, give or take a couple. The wind is so I'll be landing east to west. Be ready when I get there. I don't want any chance run-ins with a certain brother of mine you just met."

CHAPTER 12

Reggie switched off her phone, but kept it handy just in case. This car-shooting incident came as a bit of a surprise. Reggie considered herself a pretty good judge of someone's character, but she would never have figured Corbin was capable of something like this. She figured him to be the kind who might have flattened one tire in retaliation for her walking out on him, but not shooting up her whole car. This was something she might expect from a street criminal, into drugs or even worse. A feeling of uneasiness crept over her as she realized whoever did the actual shooting could still be watching her from someplace nearby. She had taken five, maybe six minutes at the most to get from the suite to her car. That hadn't given whoever did it much time. Reggie guessed that Corbin must have contacted one or more of his people as soon as she left the room, and since she hadn't heard any shots, they must have used silencers. More gangland tactics. She glanced again at the car to see holes all through the upholstery and door panels. In a way, that was good. It would mean the bullets would still be there, and it would mean Corbin could be held accountable. There wasn't much doubt he had made a tactical error this time.

She glanced around, but couldn't spot anyone watching her. Not wasting any more time, she headed out in the direction of the airstrip. In spite of her embarrassment that it was Derrick who was about to snatch her out of Corbin's grasp, it still felt good knowing she was a step ahead of Corbin. He was going to be one sorry man for crossing paths with her.

It took only minutes to reach the airstrip, where she quickly moved to the west end as Derrick had instructed. No sooner had she reached her destination than she heard the sound of an approaching plane, and seconds later she recognized it as the company Cessna. Derrick's landing was picture-perfect. She wasted no time climbing aboard, and drew a relieved breath as the plane lifted off the runway. Then, just as she expected, came the dreaded question. "You want to tell me exactly what's going on here, Regg?"

As Reggie formulated an answer, she was distracted by a glance back at the parking lot. "They're after my car with a wrecker!" she suddenly shouted.

"What?" Derrick shot back, following her gaze to see for himself.

"They plan to tow my car away! They're going to dump it into some lake or something to hide the evidence."

"Looks like you pegged that one, Regg," Derrick observed. "I talked with Clint on my way here. He contacted Quinn, who in turn contacted the police in Holbrook. There are two squad cars on the way even as we speak."

"All right for you, Quinn!" Reggie shouted. "You're a man after my own heart. You'll get my vote if you run for governor!"

"Quinn's running for governor?" Derrick asked in surprise.

"You didn't know?" she quipped. "Don't you read the papers?"

"I didn't have time to read the paper today, if that's where you got your information. And by the way, Quinn took your car being shot up pretty seriously, Regg. Clint called me back to let me know Quinn's headed this way in a police chopper to personally check it out."

Reggie glanced over at Derrick. "Be honest with me. Does this sound like something Corbin would do? I mean, that car must have taken ten to twenty hits."

"That does have me a little bothered," Derrick admitted. "It does seem a little extreme for the man. He always did have a temper, but I would never have guessed this of him."

"Well, whatever," Reggie said. "It looks like he's rocked the boat harder than he meant to."

Derrick glanced back at the tow truck heading for Reggie's Firebird. "We have to keep those guys from hauling the evidence away before the cavalry arrives," he observed. "Hang on, girl!"

An involuntary gasp hung in Reggie's throat as Derrick put the Cessna into a sudden and very steep dive in the direction of the unsuspecting wrecking crew. By the time he pulled up, they were close enough for Reggie to see the whites of the frightened men's eyes. They frantically dove for cover as the plane screamed over their heads. "Way to go, Derrick Beatty!" Reggie cried out. "Those guys should think twice before looking at my car a second time."

"I hope they get the message," Derrick said. "Actually, there's nothing I can really do but scare them."

"Looks like your bluff worked," Reggie squealed. "They're burning rubber trying to get out of the lot."

"Score one for the good guys." Derrick grinned. "I'll stay up here until the squad cars arrive, just in case. In the meantime, can you give Clint a call and let him know what's going on? He told me he'd stay in radio contact with Quinn."

Reggie checked her phone to be sure she had service from inside the Cessna. She did. Seconds later, she had Clint on the line. "What's going on, Regg?" he asked anxiously.

Reggie hurriedly brought Clint up-to-date on Derrick picking her up in the Cessna and on what was happening with her car. "Derrick tells me he's been in contact with you," she continued. "And he says you have radio contact with Sheriff Quinn."

"That's right. There are two squad cars on their way, and Quinn's in a chopper. Hang on a sec, Regina. I'll pass this latest along to Quinn now."

"Clint's making a report to Quinn," Reggie told Derrick while waiting for him to get back. "So, what the heck is this mysterious place on the map you were checking out when I called?"

"I'll tell you about that after you tell me what you were doing here at the resort, Regina Mandel. Not one second sooner."

Reggie held the phone tighter to her ear as Clint came back on. "I told Quinn everything, and he's passed it along to the men in the squad cars. Do you think it's worth going after those guys in the tow truck?"

"I don't think so, Clint," she answered. "They're not the ones who shot up my car, and they really weren't interested enough in towing it away to stick around when Derrick buzzed them. I think securing the car as evidence is what we really want."

"There!" Derrick suddenly exclaimed. "Just down the road. It's the two squad cars now."

"Looks like things are well in hand," Reggie told Clint. "The squad cars are here."

"Tell Clint we're on our way in, Regg," Derrick spoke up. "I'd like to do some more checking while I'm this close, but my fuel is running low."

Reggie nodded and passed the message along. "You two let me know when you touch down, okay?" Clint responded. "I'm one to worry about my employees at times."

"We'll let you know, Clint. Promise." She shut off the phone and glanced down just in time to see the two squad cars screaming into the lot, sirens blasting and lights flashing. They drove straight to the Firebird, and in seconds the car was surrounded by four uniformed officers. "Remind me to get those guys' names." Reggie grinned. "I'd like to send them Christmas cards this year."

Reggie leaned back and relaxed as she watched Derrick put the Cessna on a heading for home. It had been quite a day so far, and now she faced the unpleasant task of explaining to Derrick what she was doing in a meeting with his brother.

"Okay, I'm listening," Derrick said once they were on their way. "What's your story, Regg?"

A grin filled her face as she responded. "As I already told you, your brother asked me out for a lobster dinner." Reggie loved the look this brought to Derrick's face. She toyed with him another minute or so, then settled into the real story of what happened.

CHAPTER 13

When Reggie arrived at work on Monday morning, it was to find a message that Sheriff Quinn wanted to see her and Derrick in his office as soon as possible. This time there was no argument over whose car they'd use. Her Firebird was in the police compound, where it was labeled as evidence. Thoughts of it being totaled out infuriated her. She loved that car. And knowing the way insurance companies worked, she figured she'd end up with half its worth if she was lucky. The rest, she concluded, would come out of Corbin's hide.

Quinn was already in his office when Reggie and Derrick arrived. "Ah, you're here," he said, seeing them enter the room and motioning for them to sit down. "I have news. Some of it's good, and I'm afraid some's not so good. We'll start with the good. Judge Garret has issued a warrant to search the old mine. I'm in the process of organizing a crew right now. We should be able to get started by early afternoon."

"You got the warrant?" Derrick asked excitedly. "How'd that happen?"

The sheriff grinned. "Thanks to your brother's hot temper, we were able to work out a trade. He wasn't all that thrilled with the idea of our opening an investigation into your Firebird being shot up, Regg. So, with Judge Garret's help, we worked out a deal where the photographs taken of you two at the mine won't be allowed as evidence."

"You sacrificed my car to get your warrant?" Reggie quipped.

Quinn shrugged. "Hey, in this business, you learn to take what you can get. You know that, Regg."

"I know," she huffed. "But this time it's personal, and I don't like it." She looked back and forth between the two men, who were staring at her. "I'll live with it, okay?" she said. "So tell us about your plans to check out the mine."

"Not much to tell. I'm turning it over to my investigative crime unit. Those guys will go through every inch of the place. It'll be some time this afternoon when they get around to digging through the rubble you say has the back closed off."

"I want to be there for that part," Derrick said.

"I've got no problem with that. I'll let you know when I get an exact time. If everything works out right, I can run you both up there in the department chopper."

Quinn grew silent a moment before speaking again. "There's more news," he said. "We got the DNA results back on the blood samples you found at the mine."

Reggie instantly looked at Derrick to see his reaction. Whatever he was feeling, he covered it well. Quinn went on. "There's a good chance part of the blood came from your father, Derrick. We checked it against the sample of your own DNA you provided, and there's a definite biological match. If the blood wasn't your father's, it came from someone else pretty darn close. And I can only think of one person who might fit the profile."

"Corbin," Derrick stated soberly.

"Yeah. If we can get a DNA sample from him, and if it doesn't exactly match what you found in the mine, we'll know with a high degree of certainty your father met with some sort of accident there."

Derrick laughed halfheartedly. "Yeah, getting a DNA sample from Corbin ought to be pretty easy. About as easy as painting the sky red, I'd say."

"It's easier than you think," Reggie broke in, digging the fork out of her purse and handing it to Quinn. "Your lab boys will find bits of lobster and traces of butter on this fork. And," she added with a huge grin, "they'll find traces of saliva."

"Corbin's saliva?" Derrick nearly shouted. Without waiting for her answer, he stepped forward, taking her in his arms and whirling her around until it made her head spin. "Way to go, Regg!"

Reggie wasn't sure whether she liked this reaction or not. His attention was nice, but this way? She just wasn't sure.

"There's still more," Quinn continued. "The lab found the blood samples came from two people, not just one. The second was definitely no relation to you, Derrick."

"Do you have any idea who it might belong to?" Derrick asked thoughtfully.

"I was hoping you could shed some light on that question. Do you know who else would have been in the mine besides your father?"

Derrick's face lit up. "Herb Solomon!" he exclaimed. "Herb wanted Dad to analyze a new vein at the back of the mine. Dad was still planning to make the analysis the last time I talked with him."

"New vein?" Quinn asked. "I didn't know anything about that."

"Practically no one knew, Quinn. Herb needed money and was considering reopening the mine if the vein held enough promise. After Dad disappeared, Herb never spoke another word about the vein. Instead, he went to work for Corbin doing who knows what. I'm betting that if Dad's blood is down there, the other blood is Herb's." Derrick thought a moment. "I'm also betting the two of them were there when the explosion occurred."

"If we can prove that, then we'll know Herb is living with a secret," Quinn remarked. "Is there anyway we can get a DNA sample of Herb without tipping our hand by asking him outright?"

"My high school diploma," Derrick declared. "Herb attended my graduation ceremony, and when he took my diploma to look at it, he got blood on the corner. He had a cut on his finger, and the Band-Aid slipped off. I have the diploma in a frame at the house, blood splotch and all."

"Hot dog!" Quinn roared. "We're on a roll! I need that diploma now!"

CHAPTER 14

The noisy chopper blades began slowing as soon as the pilot cut power to the engine. Within seconds, it coasted to a stop. Derrick was the first one out. He turned and gave Reggie a hand down, then it was Sheriff Quinn's turn.

The quiet atmosphere Reggie had enjoyed during her first trip to the mine was gone now, replaced by the activity of dozens of investigators, each busy sifting through dirt and debris and searching for evidence. Off to one side, she noticed Corbin's security men still there, although they were powerless to do anything at the moment except observe the proceedings. Outside the mine entrance, the investigating crew had stationed a portable generator that provided electrical power for a series of lights that had been strung into the mine. There was also an air mover forcing air into the tunnel. Walking was no easier this time, but the extra light and added fresh air helped somewhat. When Reggie and Derrick arrived, the investigating crew had just finished their preliminary checks and had begun the tedious process of tunneling through the rubble at the end of the mine. As Reggie neared the scene and got her first look at their progress, she was surprised by what they had accomplished so far. The crawl hole they had tunneled was barely large enough to accommodate one man, but it already extended several feet beyond where the mine had ended the last time she was here.

"Looks like things are going good," Quinn remarked to one of the men. "What have you learned so far?"

"We've taken more samples," the man explained. "We want to be sure all this blood came from just the two we've already pinned down. We've proved the explosion was caused by only one stick of dynamite, though we found two more unexploded sticks in the debris. We're working out a timetable for when this happened. All we know so far is that it happened a long time back, and I'm talking years. We hope to have a better idea after we've had time to review all the facts. We also found the rest of the Coleman lantern to go with the piece you sent to the lab earlier. It was the old type—one that used white gas, not like the new ones that use a pressurized propane bottle. There's evidence there was a gas fire here before the explosion. Probably fueled by gas from the lantern."

"I'm through!" came a voice from the back of the tunnel where the men were working. "I've broken into another section of open tunnel."

"Come on out!" the man apparently in charge called back. "We'll want to pump some air in there before we send someone in."

Derrick stepped forward. "I want to be the one," he told the man. "I know this mine like the back of my hand, and it's my father we're looking for."

"I don't know," the man said, looking Derrick over. "Maybe we should use one of our guys."

"Which one of your men has mining experience?" Derrick pressed. "I'm the logical choice to go in, and I want to do it."

The man stood in thought for what seemed a very long time. At last he stuck out his hand. "I'm Brad Burns," he said.

Derrick accepted his handshake. "Derrick Beatty," he responded. "I practically grew up in this old hole in the ground."

"You're sure you want to do this?" Brad persisted. "If your father is in there . . ."

"I want to do it, Brad."

"Okay, buddy. Give us some time to run an air line and give you something to breathe back there."

* * *

Corbin rubbed nervously at the back of his neck as Herb looked on with obvious apprehension. The two of them were in Corbin's penthouse, where Corbin had demanded Herb meet with him. "What are they going to find in that old mine, Herb?" Corbin bellowed. "Anything that might put us in a compromising position?"

"I don't know what they're going to find, Corbin. With all this new forensic science stuff they've come up with, there's no telling what they might figure out."

Corbin slammed the palm of his hand against the wall. "Why did I ever let that woman taunt me into retaliation? And worse yet, why did I use Ramsey to do it? I didn't even know he was back on the job until he answered my call. I should have dropped it right then and there. I told him to flatten a tire, and I didn't even mean using a gun to do that. He could have removed a valve stem. But no, he shoots up her car like it was a pincushion."

"Why do you keep that man around?" Herb pressed. "He's always been bad news."

Corbin couldn't argue with that point. Ramsey had always been bad news, but never as bad as this time. Thanks to him, Corbin had been placed in a position of compromise that led to the old mine being opened to the eyes of the world, and he had no idea what the investigators might piece together down there. Maybe he would get rid of Ramsey just as soon as the problem of this other evidence was dealt with. He glanced at Herb, wondering if one more attempt at getting him off center might be in order. "How are you coming on the job at the other property?" he asked in a desperate attempt.

Herb wet his lips. "You know my feelings on that, Corbin. It's just not right."

"It's come down to the point that what's right no longer matters, Herb. We've got to get rid of it. If you can't do it, I'll send someone else who can."

"Meaning Ramsey?" Herb asked nervously.

"Meaning Ramsey!" Corbin spit back.

Herb wrung his hands nervously. "I never bargained for this sort of thing, Corbin. I was willing to go along with your plan just as long as no one got hurt in the deal. But it looks to me as though things are blowing up in your face, and I think someone is about to get hurt."

Corbin glared at Herb. "I'm paying you to keep your mouth shut, Herb. So help me, if you do anything to jeopardize our position—anything at all—I'll come down on you so hard you'll wish you'd never been born." Corbin pointed a finger at Herb. "You will keep your mouth shut. Do you understand?"

"Just as long as no one gets hurt. That's all the promise you'll get out of me, Corbin. And if you involve Ramsey, the likelihood of someone getting hurt is pretty high."

"No one's going to get hurt if we can make my brother go away before he sticks his nose in too deep. That's something I'm working on, but it's getting tougher thanks to my own stupidity. Don't you go adding to my problems, Herb. Now tell me straight. Will you get rid of the evidence, or shall I send Ramsey?"

Herb hung his head and released a painful sigh. "I'll take care of it, boss. I don't like it, but I figure I'm the one to do it if it has to be done."

"Good. I want it put to bed now, you got that?"

* * *

"Here's how we're going to do this," Brad said, checking Derrick's safety harness for a proper fit. "We're going to have a rope secured to this harness. I want you to tug on the rope every few seconds to let us know you're all right. If we don't feel your tug, we're pulling you out of there. Understood?"

"Understood," Derrick assured.

"You should have plenty of good air back there by this time, but we're not taking any chances."

Reggie wasn't sure just how safe this was, and she couldn't help wishing it was someone else crawling into the unknown blackness of that dreadful-looking hole. She held her breath as Derrick knelt in front of the opening, then, holding a powerful flashlight in front to light his way, snaked inside the cave. Just watching gave her an acute feeling of claustrophobia. His feet soon disappeared into the blackness, and all she could do was watch as the rope followed along one grueling inch at a time. "He'll be all right," Quinn told her, evidently sensing her concern. "These are professionals. They know what they're doing."

"Thanks," she whispered, never taking her eyes off the rope. She felt Quinn squeeze her arm.

"How is it in there?" Brad called.

"So far, so good," came Derrick's muffled answer.

"See anything out of the ordinary?"

"Not yet. I'm still ten feet or so from the end."

"So be honest with me," Quinn said to Reggie. "Have the two of you discussed your future at all?"

Reggie turned to stare at him. "Future?" she echoed. "What future? If you're talking about remaining partners, I guess that's a pretty sure thing. Anything else is nothing more than hearsay."

Quinn smiled and shrugged. "If you say so, Regg."

She wanted to spit fire. Why were so many people jumping to these preposterous conclusions about her and Derrick? She certainly had done nothing to encourage such thinking . . . had she?

"I'm at the end of the line," she heard Derrick call out. "Give me a minute or two to look things over."

"Do you spot anything obvious?" Brad shot back.

"Nothing obvious, but let me take a closer look."

"Use the Luminol spray and blue light," Brad instructed.

"I'm way ahead of you!" came Derrick's answer. "There's no sign of blood back here at all."

"That sounds encouraging," Quinn remarked. "I was afraid there might be a body, but it looks like I may have worried over nothing. No body means Samuel might still be alive."

"I wish," Reggie returned. "But if he's alive, where is he?"

Quinn's answer came with a possibility Reggie hadn't thought of. "Maybe somewhere in the facility Derrick spotted from the air yesterday before he picked you up at the resort?"

"Yeah," she reasoned. "Maybe so."

"I've been after Derrick to let me send some guys out there to check it out, but he refuses to tell me its exact location. Says he wants to check it himself. I could force the issue I guess, but . . ."

"But Samuel's his father, right?"

"Right."

"Take up the slack in the rope. I'm coming out," came Derrick's voice out of the darkness.

Reggie breathed a sigh of relief minutes later when his head appeared through the opening. Three of the men pulled him the rest of the way out, then helped take him off the safety harness. "So, what's your report?" Brad asked.

"Nothing there but the end of a very old mine," Derrick said. "I did find this, though." He held out his hand, revealing a solid gold nugget about the size of an apricot seed. "There's definitely another rich vein there for the taking."

Reggie moved forward for a better look. "It's beautiful," she said. "I've never seen a real gold nugget before."

Brad scratched his head. "This requires some thought. Is the nugget evidence or just your good fortune?"

Quinn entered the conversation. "The way I see it, the nugget belongs with the mine. If Corbin ever learns Derrick has it, I suppose he might ask him for it. But I'm not about to tell Corbin that Derrick has it."

Brad laughed. "Sound reasoning if ever I heard it. Put the nugget in your pocket, Derrick. You deserve it for being the one to crawl back there."

"This is one time I can't say I'm disappointed at coming up empty-handed." He glanced at the nugget, then back at the others. "Evidence wise I mean." This brought a laugh from the group.

"We knew what you meant," Reggie said, moving closer to Derrick. "I'm so glad you didn't find something back there you didn't want to find. And I'm glad you're out of there in one piece." On an impulse, she gave him a quick peck on the cheek. "You're a very brave man, Derrick. I'm proud to have you as my partner."

Derrick touched his face where she had kissed him and smiled. "And I'm proud to have you as my partner. I'll fight the man who claims to have a prettier one." She couldn't help blushing, but hearing him say it was worth the embarrassment.

* * *

Corbin closed the door behind Herb, then crossed the room to the large glass doors overlooking the section of resort behind the hotel as well as the lake. Corbin loved the view from his penthouse. Overlooking his empire, which stretched as far as the eye could see, gave him a sense of power. Corbin had always known that Herb Solomon was the weak link in the chain binding the empire, and that was rapidly becoming more evident. Of all the problems facing Corbin over this unpleasant turn of events, the problem of how to handle Herb was the most pressing. Perhaps, he thought, Herb should be sent away some-place. Maybe to the Caribbean or someplace equally as remote. It would mean upping the ante Corbin was already investing to keep Herb's mouth closed, but it might be worth it. He'd give it some more thought, but for now he wanted Herb watched. And like it or not, he would have to leave that chore to Ramsey Borden. Corbin removed his cell phone and stared at it. Yes, it was definitely time to bring Ramsey in. He made the call.

CHAPTER 15

It was two days following the investigation into the old mine before Reggie and Derrick heard anything back from Quinn. During this time, they remained busy on another hot case involving threatening phone calls to Jim Boyd, the manager of a local bank. Jim felt the police weren't doing everything possible on the case, so he enlisted Banister as a backup. It took some legwork, but Reggie and Derrick soon had a handle on things. When they learned that Mrs. Boyd had been harassed by a stalker some years back, it was the lead they needed to break the case open. The stalker, a man named Rudy Fitzgerald, had recently been paroled from state prison, where he had served seven years on an unrelated charge. All it took was one search warrant, and they had their man. Rudy, it seems, was a man who believed in keeping a journal of everything he did, including his calls to Jim Boyd. As things worked out, it was while Reggie and Derrick were presenting their evidence against Fitzgerald to Quinn that Quinn reciprocated by filling them in on everything he had on Samuel's case.

Reggie wasn't surprised when she learned that Derrick's suspicions about part of the blood in the mine belonging to Herb Solomon were on the mark. Neither was she all that surprised that the DNA sample from Corbin's fork didn't match the DNA from the second sample of blood found in the mine. All indications were that the blood did in fact belong to Samuel Beatty. "What about a time frame?" she asked after listening to

Quinn's account. "Was the crime scene crew able to pinpoint when the explosion occurred in the mine?"

Quinn nodded. "They did, and their time frame fits perfectly with Samuel's disappearance. We're on to something big here. I feel it in these old bones."

"All right!" Derrick broke in. "How soon can you bring Herb Solomon in for questioning?"

"I'd have him here now if I could find him. I have a warrant out, but no one seems to know his whereabouts at the moment. And that includes your brother, Corbin."

"That figures." Derrick responded. "Corbin probably hid Herb when he learned we were digging around for information. Corbin knows where he is. You can bet on it."

"How about your dad?" Reggie asked. "Are you betting Corbin knows where *he* is?"

Derrick thought a moment. "Yeah, Corbin knows where Dad is. I'm positive of that much. What I don't know is whether Dad is alive or . . ."

"Is Corbin the sort who would have killed his own father?" Quinn asked soberly.

"No," Derrick stated emphatically. "Corbin's a lot of things, but a murderer isn't one of them. He couldn't kill Dad or anyone else."

Quinn brushed a hand across his mouth. "Okay, then is Corbin the sort who could hide the whereabouts of your dad's remains if he thought it would be to his advantage?"

Again, Derrick had to think. "I have a hard time accepting that he could even do that. Maybe, but I strongly doubt it. I come closer to believing Dad is alive someplace. It could be he was badly injured in the mine explosion and Corbin has him in a rest home. Maybe not even in our state. I just don't know."

"Maybe you're on to something, Derrick," Reggie suggested. "There is the distinct possibility your dad is in a rest home, or he could be someplace closer. Like the facilities you discovered from the air last Saturday. Maybe it's time we checked out those facilities."

"If anyone checks out those facilities, it should be my men," Quinn said. "All I need is an exact location, and I'll send some people there in a hurry."

Derrick shook off this idea. "Not to be obstinate, Sheriff, but I want to be the one who checks out those facilities. Your men would need a warrant, and we'd be right back in a legal battle with Corbin. I can have 'engine trouble' in the Cessna and be forced to land at the place. And I agree with Regg. Now's the time to move—before Corbin finds a way to cover up whatever might be out there."

"It could be a trap, you know," Quinn pointed out. "The way you got your hands on the map showing the location is a bit questionable. You could be playing right into Corbin's hands with a stunt like you propose."

"It's a chance I'll have to take, Sheriff. If there's something at that place that will lead me to Dad, then I've got to find it."

"I don't know," Quinn persisted. "It's awfully risky. At least give me the location to the place so I can back you up if you get in trouble."

"I'll compromise with you," Derrick relented. "As soon as I have the Cessna on the ground, I'll radio you the location."

Quinn shrugged. "If that's the best deal I can get, then I'll take it. Just don't go back on your word, okay?"

"I'll make the call myself," Reggie interjected. "You know you can trust me, Sheriff."

This brought looks of concern from both men. "You won't be going with me, Regg," Derrick insisted. "This is something I have to do alone."

Reggie was sure this little obstacle was coming, but she wasn't about to be excluded. "Not on your life, Mr. Beatty. I'm your partner, and I will not be treated as anything less. We do this together, end of discussion."

"Regg, I . . ."

She raised a finger. "End of discussion, Mr. Beatty!"

"I think she means it," Quinn remarked through a cheeky grin. "And if you think she's hard to deal with now, just wait till you're married to her."

Reggie opened her mouth to blast Quinn, but she realized from the look on Derrick's face that Quinn's statement had disarmed him. She decided to let it go, figuring that sometimes winning a war came with the price of losing a battle.

* * *

Sheriff Quinn waited all of thirty seconds after Derrick and Reggie stepped out the door before calling Officer Rossland into his office. "What's up, Sheriff?" she asked, entering the room.

"Get ahold of my chopper pilot, Brenda. Have him pick me up as soon as he can get here. I need to make a trip to Snowflake ASAP. Contact the police department at Snowflake to let them know I'm on my way. And one more thing—have all my calls transferred to my cell phone so I can take them on location."

"Snowflake?" Brenda asked. "What's going on in Snowflake?"

The sheriff quickly explained about Derrick and Reggie's plans to check out the suspicious facilities he reasoned must be somewhere in the vicinity of Snowflake. "I won't know the exact location of the place until they call," he continued. "But when I do get the call, I darn sure don't want to be as far away as Mesa. And, just so you know, I don't plan on waiting an hour to make my move, either."

Brenda laughed. "Are you saying you had your fingers crossed when you made Derrick the promise?"

"I didn't promise anything—not exactly anyway. I may have hinted a little something, but if that makes me a liar, then so be it. There's no way of knowing what danger those kids are walking into."

CHAPTER 16

"This is the place," Derrick said, pointing out the window of the Cessna to the facilities below them. "What do you make of it, Regg?"

She studied it closely. There was a landing strip, two buildings, a water tower, and the whole place was closed off with high, chain-link fencing. Another thing she noticed were the power lines bringing in electricity and telephone connections. This meant it wasn't completely isolated from the outside. "I'm not sure what to make of it," she responded. "But I agree that we need a closer look."

"Do you still have that tracking device in your purse?" Derrick asked.

"I do, and it's turned on. How about yours?"

"Strapped to my belt and turned on."

"Shall I make that call to Quinn now?" she asked.

"Yeah, but make sure he knows to give us a full hour. If he hasn't heard from us by then, he has my blessing to move in."

Reggie was just finishing up her call as the Cessna touched down. Derrick taxied to a point near the larger of the two buildings and cut the engine. "Looks like some sort of warehouse," Reggie observed.

Derrick nodded. "That would be my guess."

Reggie examined the building closely. The side facing them contained large double doors in the center, and a smaller door on one end appeared to be the entrance to a small office. All the doors were closed. There was also a window where she estimated the office to be. This was blocked by shades hanging on the inside. Glancing at the second building, which was located only a short distance from the first, she concluded this one was probably used as a residence. "So, what's the plan?" she asked.

Derrick didn't answer right away, as he too was studying everything closely. "I think I'll start by checking the smaller building," he said. "I want you in the plane with your cell phone handy. If anything looks unusual, call Quinn ASAP."

Reggie frowned as she contemplated what he was asking. "Still trying to keep me out of the action, I see."

"Come on, Regg! Be reasonable! I need you here maintaining communications while I look things over. Being a backup doesn't mean you're out of the action."

Reggie's jaw tightened as she watched Derrick step out of the Cessna and climb to the ground. "If anything goes wrong— anything at all—make that call," he instructed. "And if you think it's something I haven't noticed, find a way to get my attention."

"Like how?" she asked sarcastically. "They don't put horns on Cessnas."

"I'll keep my cell phone on vibrate. You know my number."

Reggie leaned back in her seat and watched in disgust as Derrick made his way cautiously toward the smaller building. He was treating her like a child, and she didn't like it one bit. When he reached the building, she could tell he found the door to be locked. Yet she knew that to him, this was only a small setback. Sure enough, he had the door open in a matter of seconds and disappeared inside. It wasn't until he was out of sight that the magnitude of what he might run into hit her. This only served to intensify her feeling that she was not doing her part by sitting here in the Cessna. She glanced again at the larger building. Who was Derrick to tell her what to do in a situation like this anyway? He was her partner, not her supervisor.

Reggie's attention was drawn to the smaller door leading to what appeared to be an office. Logic told her it would be locked, just as the one Derrick had checked. She didn't have Derrick's skill at picking locks, but this door didn't look all that difficult. She stepped out onto the wing for a better look. She was almost sure the door could be opened with a credit card. After a quick glance around revealed nothing unusual, she stepped to the ground and made her way to the door. Derrick wouldn't like this, but what did she care? She wanted in on the excitement, and the excitement wasn't to be found in the front seat of the Cessna.

She tried the knob, and sure enough, it was locked. Pulling a credit card from her purse, she shoved it in the space between the door and the jamb. She smiled in satisfaction as she felt the latch give way. "Take that, Derrick Beatty," she whispered to herself as she pushed the door open. "I can get through locked doors too, when I put my mind to it."

One glance inside told her she had been right—this was an office. There was a desk at the back of the room with one file cabinet next to it. She also noticed an inside door leading into what was apparently the main room of the warehouse. Cautiously, she eased her way inside, only to discover she had made a monumental mistake. It would have been impossible for her to have spotted the man crouching against the wall just inside the doorway in time to ward off his attack. A cold chill gripped her as she found herself in his clutches with his hand clasped over her mouth, preventing her from uttering a sound.

"Hold it right there, missy!" the assailant commanded. "Just behave yourself and no one gets hurt!"

It took only seconds to realize that struggling against this powerful man was fruitless. And adding to her plight was the appearance of a second man entering the room through the door leading to the warehouse. This man had a pistol in his hand. After taking a few seconds to evaluate the situation, he spoke, addressing Reggie directly. "My partner's going to remove his hand. Not one sound out of you, you hear?"

Reggie attempted to nod. It was enough to get the message across. Slowly the man removed his hand from her mouth, but not his grip on her. The man with the gun moved in closer. "Are you the one who flew that plane in here?" he demanded.

Reggie's heart pounded, and her mind raced frantically. Thoughts of her shot-up car didn't help. If these were the men behind that, there was no telling what she might be in for now. She took a quick breath and tried to calm herself. In spite of her concern, she had to remain level-headed. Maybe these men hadn't seen Derrick. Maybe they thought she was alone. All she could do was play along with this idea and silently pray for a miracle. "I was running low on fuel," she said, hoping they wouldn't notice the trembling in her voice. "I spotted the landing strip and set down. I was hoping to find a phone so I could call for help."

The man with the gun pulled her purse from her shoulder and rummaged through it. "Why would you need to find a phone when you have one of your own?" he sneered, holding up her cell phone. She held her breath, hoping he'd overlook the tracking device. Fortunately, it was small, and she had crammed it into a side pocket that he hadn't bothered to open.

"I tried using my cell phone," she said, maintaining her ploy. "It showed this to be a nonservice area." She prayed he wouldn't check the phone for himself, as this would be easy to disprove. To her relief, he shoved the phone into his pocket and dropped her purse to the floor. "What do we do now, Ramsey?" the man gripping her asked.

Ramsey ran a hand through his hair. "I don't know, Blake. Much as I hate doing this, I suppose I better check with Corbin. He *is* the one who pays the bills."

Ramsey and Blake, Reggie reasoned to herself. At least she could attach names to these culprits now.

The sound of skin against a day's growth of whiskers reached Reggie's ears as the man called Ramsey rubbed his chin. "What's your name, lady?" he asked gruffly.

She had to think fast. It would be easy for these men to identify her by searching her purse further—something she most definitely didn't want. If Ramsey was going to call Corbin, as he had indicated he might, her name would be instantly recognized. What was she to do? It appeared she had little choice but to tell the truth and hope for the best. "Reggie," she answered. "Reggie Mandel. If you call Corbin Beatty, he'll know me."

This brought a look of surprise to Ramsey's face. "You're acquainted with Corbin?" he asked. "How so?"

"Very casually, I assure you," she responded. "Would you mind putting that gun away and telling your partner here to let go of my arm?"

Ramsey stared at her a moment longer, then signaled Blake to release her. He then holstered his gun and picked up the phone from the desk behind him. Rubbing the soreness from her arm, Reggie watched him make the call. In the time it took for Corbin to answer, she closely examined her surroundings. She drew a quick breath as she peered through the open door leading into the warehouse to see a helicopter parked there. Who were these men, and what was going on here? If Samuel Beatty was on these premises, he must have been in the building Derrick had gone into.

"Corbin?" Ramsey said into the phone. "Ramsey here. We're at the property, and we've encountered a problem."

Corbin's answer was loud enough for Reggie to hear. "Problem? What problem?"

"Blake and I got here about half an hour ago. We pulled the chopper into the warehouse the way you wanted. We were just about to go looking for Herb when we heard the noise of an approaching plane."

"Plane?" Corbin asked.

"Yeah. And it set down right here. By the time Blake and me got to where we could see, we spotted this woman breaking into the office. Says her name's Reggie Mandel. Claims you know her."

"Reggie Mandel's at the property?" Corbin grew silent for several seconds. "Any sign of a man with her?" he barked.

"We didn't spot no one else."

"What about the evidence I sent you there to check on? Did Herb do his job? Is it gone?"

Evidence? Reggie thought. *What evidence could he be talking about?*

"Nothing's been touched," Ramsey explained. "If Herb's here, we haven't spotted him yet. But what about this lady? What do we do with her, Corbin?"

"Let me think," Corbin shot back apprehensively. "I need to talk to her. I guess you'd better bring her to me. But not to the resort. Bring her out to the island. I'll meet you there near the boat dock."

Reggie felt her skin crawl as she realized what this meant. Corbin wanted her brought to the small island she had seen from the air when she and Derrick passed over it in the Cessna. There wouldn't be any witnesses there. Was her life in danger? She didn't know, but the pounding in her heart didn't let up in the least.

"We'll be there in a half hour," Ramsey said.

"Listen, Ramsey!" Corbin shouted before Ramsey could hang up. "No rough stuff with this lady, you understand?"

Ramsey laughed. "You know me, Corbin. You say no rough stuff, then that's what you get."

"I mean it, Ramsey! Not one hair on her head out of place! You got that?"

Ramsey rolled his eyes and hung up the phone. "Did you get that, Blake?" He smirked. "Not one hair on the lady's head out of place."

Reggie's eyes shifted between these two men. Her greatest concern came from the one called Ramsey. She realized she might be better off to get a bluff in with this man rather than just going along like a quiet little mouse. Bolstering her courage, she spoke. "It sounds to me like we're talking kidnap here. That's pretty heavy stuff, misters. Are you sure you want to be a party to this?"

"That's Corbin's problem," Ramsey growled. "I only work for the man. I caught you trespassing on private property. If he wants to talk to you about it, who am I to argue?"

"At least let me call someone about my plane," she schemed, having little hope her ploy would work but trying anyway.

"Your plane will be fine where it is until Corbin decides what to do with it. Do you plan on coming along quietly, or do I have to pretend I didn't hear those last orders?"

Reggie grabbed her purse. At least she had the tracking device going for her. She knew the other half of the device used as the finder was in the Cessna. When Derrick realized something was wrong, it wouldn't take him long to be hot on her trail. "I'll go quietly," she answered. "But don't think I plan to overlook this little episode. Your path and mine will cross again. Next time, it'll be on my terms."

Fire blazed in Ramsey's eyes. He moved in very close as if to say something, but just stood staring at her. At last he turned and headed out the door into the warehouse. "Bring her along," he shot back to Blake without turning to look.

* * *

Derrick pushed open the door and stepped inside the building. It was definitely a residence. Closing the door behind him, he made his way into the living room. He found it filled with all the normal things—furniture, a television, lamps, even a telephone. But from the presence of all the dust, it was obvious the place hadn't been lived in for some time. Moving on to the kitchen, Derrick opened the refrigerator, which he found empty except for a couple of bottles of Sparklets drinking water.

In the bathroom he found a razor, blades, shampoo, toothbrush and toothpaste, combs, and deodorant. But again, none of these things appeared to have been used recently. If he expected to find any answers in this place, he wasn't sure where they were going to come from. Suddenly he heard someone behind him. "Glad to see you could make it, Derrick. I knew you wouldn't let me down when I had that map sent your way."

Derrick spun to find himself face to face with a man he hadn't seen in years. "Herb Solomon?" he gasped. "You're the one who sent the drunk guy with the map?"

"Sorry for not giving you a better welcome, but I had to be sure we weren't being watched before I made myself known. I'm sure your brother knows by now I've double-crossed him. There are a couple of his dupes here on the property, and I have no doubt they're looking for me. They won't find me, though. I know my way around this place well enough to stay a step ahead of them."

"Herb! What are you talking about? Are you saying there's someone else here besides you?"

"Yeah. Over at the warehouse. Corbin sent them here to do a job he knows I'm not going to do. There's some evidence he wants disposed of."

"I didn't see a car when I flew in," Derrick remarked, more concerned about Reggie at the moment than about whatever evidence it was Herb was referring to.

"They flew in in a chopper. It's inside the warehouse, which is why you didn't see it. Me, I got here on a motorcycle, which I hid next door."

"Herb!" Derrick pressed. "I'm not alone either. My partner flew in with me. She's in the Cessna. Will she be in any danger there?"

Herb paled. "You have a partner with you? That's not good, Derrick. Yes, she could be in trouble. One of the guys Corbin sent out here is Ramsey Borden. That guy's definitely dangerous. He's nuts."

Suddenly their conversation was interrupted by what sounded like gunshots. Derrick broke for the front door with Herb hot on his heels.

* * *

Even before they reached the chopper, Reggie had the one called Blake pegged as the pilot. Ramsey was more of a muscle man. Her theory proved right. Once she and Blake were inside the chopper, Ramsey moved to the doors, where he pressed a button, opening them electrically. Blake started the engine and taxied the craft out through the doors. That's when Reggie heard the gunshots. A glance in the direction of the Cessna told her what had happened. Ramsey had shot out both tires. "Why did he do that, Blake?" she shouted. "Corbin never gave that order. I would have heard."

"You have to understand the way Ramsey thinks," Blake explained. "He can get a little crazy. What you said to him back there in the office didn't sit well, I'm afraid. You're better off keeping quiet. Once you're with Corbin, you'll be okay, but I can't guarantee anything with Ramsey. Just pay attention to what I say, and play the part."

Shooting out the tires on the Cessna threw a wrench in Reggie's plan. How could Derrick follow them now even if the tracker in her purse did point the way? Reggie was in deep trouble this time, and she knew it.

* * *

Derrick made it outside just in time to see a chopper lifting off. He could clearly make out Reggie inside. Wasting no time, he headed for the Cessna. He was still several feet away when he realized what the shots he heard earlier had meant. Both tires had been flattened. Yanking out his cell phone, he started punching in Quinn's number, only to realize the battery was dead. How could he have let that happen? And of all times, why now? His first thought was to use the radio in the Cessna, but then he remembered seeing a phone inside the house. A phone would be faster than the radio, as using the radio would require a go-between. He turned to see Herb just now reaching him. "I saw a phone in the house, Herb! Is it connected?"

"No!" Herb shouted. "The phones here are useless to you. They're a direct line to Corbin's penthouse at the resort, and that's it. But I have a better plan. Come on! We have no time to lose!"

"No, wait! Let me make a call on the radio!"

"Listen to me, Derrick! There's no time for that! I know what I'm doing!"

Derrick was shocked to see Herb break into a run for the warehouse. His only thought was the motorcycle Herb had said he rode here. A motorcycle wasn't much, but it was better than nothing. Derrick glanced back at the Cessna, thinking again about the radio, but he finally figured the radio would be there if whatever Herb had in mind didn't work. He hurriedly followed after Herb.

As they passed through the open doors into the warehouse, Herb kept right on running toward the far end of the building. When he finally did stop, he was so out of breath all he could do was stand there gasping for air. "I'm too old for this," he finally choked out. Then, pointing to a large object in front of where he stood, he managed to say, "Here's our transportation, Derrick. Pull off the tarp."

Derrick stared in confusion. Whatever this was, it wasn't the motorcycle. It was too large for that. Grabbing one corner of the covering, he gave it a yank. As it pulled away, Derrick got his first glimpse of what lay beneath. He stood frozen, instantly recognizing what it was. "HERB!" he shrieked yanking the tarp the rest of the way off. "AM I SEEING THINGS, OR IS THIS REAL?"

Herb was still fighting for his breath, but he could at least speak now. "This is the evidence Corbin wanted me to get rid of, Derrick. Now maybe you can appreciate why I couldn't do it."

Derrick stared at the object. He had never seen anything more beautiful in his life. "Dad's plane has been right here all these years?" he gasped.

"Only because I refused to allow your brother to dispose of it. Your dad loved this old bird. I just couldn't bring myself to let Corbin destroy it."

Derrick's mind was racing. "Is it flyable, Herb?" he cried out.

"You bet it's flyable. I've kept it in perfect condition all these years. It's full of fuel and ready to go."

"You kept it flyable?" Derrick asked in disbelief.

"With the help of a good friend who just happens to be a mechanic," Herb explained. "Someone I never told your brother about. Let's get these doors open and shove it outside."

Derrick raced to remove the wheel chalks while Herb opened the motorized doors at the end of the warehouse. With one man on each wing, they had the little craft outside the building in less than two minutes. "There's something I have to get out of the Cessna," Derrick shouted. "Can you get this thing started, Herb?"

"I can do that. Can't fly it, but I can start it."

As Herb climbed into the front cockpit, Derrick made a beeline for the Cessna, where he grabbed the tracking half of the electronic device that could pinpoint Reggie's location—if she still had her part of the tracker turned on. A quick check found it was working and pointing southwest. "They're headed for the resort," Derrick said to himself. Just then, he heard the engine on the old biplane fire up. It was like music to his ears. There were lots of questions that needed answers, but first he had to catch that chopper.

When Derrick reached the plane, he quickly climbed into the rear cockpit, where he strapped himself in and put on his headphones. "Can you hear me, Herb?" he barked into the mike.

"Loud and clear. Do you have any idea where they've taken her?"

"I'd say they're headed for the resort."

"That figures. Let's get this old bird in the air." That was a suggestion Derrick didn't need to hear twice.

CHAPTER 17

When Reggie's call came telling Sheriff Quinn the location of the facilities, he was way ahead of the game. He had lined up four backup officers in two separate squad cars who would accompany him to the scene. As it worked out, the actual location was somewhat farther from Snowflake than Quinn had anticipated. Even with lights flashing and sirens blaring, it still took forty-seven minutes to reach their destination. Jumping from his car before it rolled to a full stop, Quinn headed straight for the locked gate to see what he was up against. That's when he spotted the Cessna.

"I knew it!" he shouted back to the others. "Bring the bolt cutters! We can forget a warrant! That Cessna with flattened tires is all the probable cause we need."

One of the officers stepped up with the cutters and had the chain off within seconds. Quinn ordered the other officers to check out the buildings while he headed straight for the Cessna. "Just as I feared," he said, examining the first tire. "A gunshot did this. And we have a bullet lodged in the soft asphalt that could help identify the one who pulled the trigger."

Removing his pocketknife, Quinn carefully dug out the bullet and wrapped it in his handkerchief. "I'm betting this little fellow came from the same gun as the one used to shoot up Reggie's car," he muttered to himself. He checked the other tire. It too had been flattened with a bullet, but this one seemed to have ricocheted away.

Quinn stood and glanced at the two buildings the other officers were now searching. He had no idea what had happened
here, but he was betting whatever it was wouldn't be good. He
was also betting Derrick and Reggie were no longer on the
premises. One thing was for sure—a thorough search of this
place was in order.

It was quickly evident that Quinn was right about Derrick
and Reggie. They were nowhere to be found. One unusual thing
Quinn noticed was that the large doors at each end of the
building had been left standing wide open. There were also fresh
tracks in the dust on each end, indicating vehicles had recently
been parked there. The tire tracks on the north end appeared to
have come from a light plane, while the skid tracks on the south
end resembled something made by a helicopter. One of the officers also stumbled onto a Kawasaki street bike hidden behind a
pile of old tires on the north end of the warehouse.

"Get on the horn!" Quinn instructed the senior officer.
"Find out if anyone close by has spotted a light plane or a
chopper within the past hour!"

"I'm on it, Sheriff," the officer said, beelining it for his patrol
car.

I'm not sure what's going on here, Quinn pondered to himself.
*But I'm betting Corbin Beatty is behind whatever it is. If either one
of those kids is hurt, Corbin will wish he'd never heard the name
Ed Quinn. Bet on it!*

CHAPTER 18

This was nearly unbelievable. Derrick had not only found his father's old biplane, he actually had it in the air again. Even in his wildest dreams he would never have pictured himself in the cockpit of the N3N-3 again. No plane he'd ever flown matched the ease and control of this one. It was like finding an old friend. But what did this mean about his father's fate? Was this a good omen, or was it evidence Samuel might never be found? Derrick just didn't know. One thing he did know—the tracking device in Reggie's purse was working perfectly. It was still guiding him on a southwesterly direction, exactly what he would expect if she were being taken to the resort. He estimated she was about fifteen minutes ahead of them. Keying his microphone, he spoke to Herb. "Tell me what's going on. You've known the whereabouts of this old plane the whole time, haven't you?"

"Listen, Derrick," Herb stumbled. "I'm not proud of what I've done, but I have known about it, yes. I wouldn't have come forward even now if it weren't for your brother's decision to get rid of the plane once and for all."

"How did the plane get there in the first place, Herb? And where is my father?"

Herb sighed loudly. "You are aware of my gambling problem, right?" he asked.

"I know you did have a problem. I was hoping you might have licked it by this time."

"I'm doing better now, Derrick. But it's not easy. I got myself in pretty deep just about the time Samuel shut down the mining operation. Samuel came up with the suggestion I reopen the mine on my own. He offered to put up the necessary financing, just like I did for him once. He was positive there was an untapped vein just sitting there waiting for the taking. He offered to help me evaluate its worth, something I didn't have the savvy to do myself."

"All that I knew, Herb. The last time I saw Dad, the two of us flew up there to check the mine for you, but we got sidetracked."

"There's one thing you probably don't know, Derrick. I went to Corbin and asked his help in opening the mine."

Herb was right. Derrick didn't know about this bit of news. "Why would you do that, Herb?"

"You have to understand, Derrick. I know next to nothing about mining. I was your dad's partner in name only. Oh, I made an appearance at the place every now and then, you know, just to see how things were going, but that's about it. You and Corbin worked with your dad long enough to get a handle on how he ran things, so if I was going to reopen the mine, you were the logical ones I'd look to for help."

"And you chose Corbin over me?"

"Be honest, Derrick. What would you have said if I had approached you about reopening the mine? Your interest at the time was in your job at the agency."

"You're right," Derrick agreed. "I probably would have turned you down."

"That's what I figured. Corbin, on the other hand, was down on his luck in those days."

"Enough so that he actually considered working the old mine?" Derrick asked, shocked at the thought. "Corbin hated that mine—everything about it."

"He wasn't going to work the mine personally," Herb explained. "He was going to hire a good foreman, get a working crew together, then oversee the operation from a comfortable distance. It would have been my responsibility to set up an office at the location and keep a closer eye on things."

"Uh-huh. And how much was my brother's help going to cost you, Herb?"

"He wanted fifty percent of the take. But what choice did I have? Without him I would have been up a creek. The whole thing was contingent on the vein proving rich enough to be worth it, naturally."

"Did Dad know Corbin was in on the deal when he agreed to finance you, Herb?"

"No, I never told your dad that part. I was afraid to. I wasn't sure how he'd take the news."

"Well you should have been, Herb. And speaking of Dad, what exactly do you know about him?"

"I'm getting there, Derrick, don't rush me. After I made the deal with Corbin, I went back to your dad and pressured him into coming up to the mine with me to evaluate the new vein. We flew there on a Saturday, a week after the two of you were there."

Derrick was growing impatient. "The explosion, Herb!" he pressed. "How did it happen?"

"We started into the mine," Herb explained. "I was carrying a Coleman lantern and three sticks of dynamite. Samuel planned on using the dynamite to blast open the new vein for a better look at it. The new vein was all the way at the back of the mine. We were almost there when I stumbled over a rock. The lantern fell from my hand and burst into a ball of flame. I jumped back in panic, and in my haste I dropped the dynamite. One stick landed near the lantern, and the fuse caught fire."

Herb grew silent a moment before going on. At last he continued. "I was scared half out of my skin, Derrick. I just froze. By the time your dad realized what was happening, it was too late to extinguish the fuse. He dove for me in a flying tackle and forced me against the rocky floor." Herb sighed at the memory. "He covered me with his own body, Derrick. I heard the explosion, then everything went black. It was two days later that I woke up at old Doc Pepperton's house."

"Doc Pepperton?" Derrick shouted. "That old drunk? How did you get there, Herb? Was my dad with you?"

"It seems Corbin was a little anxious to learn if Samuel was going to put up the money. Without telling me, he drove to the mine that day to watch us from behind a stand of trees." Herb paused to laugh halfheartedly. "Was that good luck for Samuel and me or was it the beginning of our undoing?"

"Corbin saved your life?" Derrick asked.

"Without him, both of us might have died, right there on the spot. Fortunately for us, he heard the explosion and rushed inside looking for us. He drug us out one at a time and drove us down the hill to old Doc Pepperton's place."

"That makes no sense!" Derrick exclaimed. "Why didn't he call 911 and get some real professional help, Herb?"

"I don't think Corbin knew how bad we were hurt. He tells me I was awake and talking to him, though I don't remember a thing about it. Even Doc Pepperton misjudged how bad your dad was hurt. He figured we'd both recover in a day or so. He was right in my case, but your dad wasn't so lucky."

"Get to the point, Herb!" Derrick persisted. "What happened to Dad?"

"You're not going to like where this is headed, Derrick."

From the back cockpit, Derrick could just make out the top of Herb's head in the front cockpit. Derrick thought about doing a barrel roll or some other violent maneuver to shake some sense into that head, but he soon realized the futility of the idea. If he gave Herb a heart attack, he might never learn his father's fate. "Get on with the story, Herb!" Derrick again demanded.

Again there was an aggravating pause before Herb continued. "Well," he said at last, "it soon became apparent your dad wasn't coming around like Pepperton expected him to. Pepperton wanted to get your dad to a hospital where he could be checked out properly. By this time I'd recovered my capabilities enough to know pretty well what was going on. I agreed with Pepperton."

"Are you hinting that Corbin was willing to let Dad die, rather than get him to a hospital?" Derrick had a hard time believing his brother could stoop so low.

"Corbin wanted to help his dad, but he had something else in mind at the same time. He figured if Samuel didn't make it, he had to protect his own personal interests. Are you aware your dad had a will made out before any of this happened?"

"He mentioned a will, yes. I never saw it. I didn't figure I had any reason to."

"Yeah, well, as his partner I was allowed to read it. He had it updated at the time the resort was being constructed. Some things were to be divided between you and Corbin, but you were the one to inherit Beatty Enterprises. Saint that your dad always was, he even left old Herb pretty well taken care of in the will. I made the mistake of telling Corbin about it and that I knew where Samuel kept it. It was in a desk drawer at his new office in the resort hotel. Corbin broke into the office and stole it. That's when he came up with the idea of sending Samuel to California, where he could get the medical help he needed under an assumed name."

"What?" Derrick bellowed. "How could he get away with a thing like that?"

"He did it with Pepperton's help. Pepperton had connections in California. He was able to check Samuel into the Community Hospital in San Bernardino under the name of another patient Pepperton once treated there. It was touch and go, but Pepperton pulled it off on the promise he'd be recompensed with a healthy sum if Corbin did inherit Samuel's fortune."

"That's when Corbin came up with the fake will," Derrick guessed.

"I'm ashamed to admit that all three of us were in on it. Corbin pulled in a couple of lawyer friends of his and made up a new will leaving everything to you-know-who. I was to come out of the deal with my gambling debts paid. I hope you understand how desperate I was, Derrick. I was in so deep I was looking at being dumped in the ocean with concrete shoes on my feet if I didn't pay up soon. As for Pepperton, he was promised a hundred grand. Things went even better than expected when Samuel came around enough for Pepperton to trick him into signing the fake will."

Derrick's grip tightened on the control stick at hearing Herb say he believed the signature on the fake will was Samuel's. So that's the way it happened. Pepperton had led Herb and the others to believe the signature was Samuel's, when in fact, he knew it wasn't. That made sense. If Pepperton got his promised money out of the deal, what did he care about the others? If the will was later proved a fraud, it was no skin off his nose. But, if that was how it happened, did it really mean Samuel was alive when the signature was faked, or was it done after Pepperton knew it was too late to ever get a real signature? A scary thought.

"One thing to my credit," Herb said, moving away from the subject of Samuel's final fate, which Derrick realized Herb was having a hard time disclosing. "I did see to it this old biplane was taken care of. Corbin wanted to dispose of it early on, but I talked him out of it. I personally saw to it that the plane was dismantled and hidden inside a trailer on an eighteen wheeler until we could find a more permanent hiding place for it."

Derrick was suddenly distracted from Herb's story when a glance at the tracking instrument told him it had stopped moving. The chopper must have landed, and if it did, all indications still pointed to it being at the resort. According to Derrick's calculations, his estimate of being fifteen minutes behind the chopper was just about right, as that's about how much longer it would take him to reach the resort in the little biplane.

CHAPTER 19

Reggie looked on nervously as the pilot eased the chopper down on the soft beach sand near the boat dock where Corbin stood waiting. "This is your stop," Ramsey shouted, opening the door and motioning for Reggie to step out of the chopper.

She glared at him. "You haven't heard the last of me!" she shouted back to be heard over the noise of the idling chopper. "I know you're the one behind the shooting up of my Firebird, and I loved that car!"

"That was your car?" Ramsey asked. "I should have guessed."

"One way or another, you *will* pay for that mistake, Ramsey. You can take that to the bank!"

Ramsey pointed a finger in her face. "Don't make idle threats at me, woman! There's no place big enough for you to hide if I decide to find you, and I *will* find you if you ever cross me. Now get out of the chopper!"

There was more Reggie wanted to say, but she bit her tongue and let it go. Stepping to the ground, she stared into the eyes of Corbin Beatty, who was there to greet her. Her fears were lessened now that she was out of Ramsey's hands. She honestly didn't believe Corbin presented any great danger.

The wind from the chopper blades gusted past them as the chopper lifted off and moved quickly on a course opposite the one it took to get there. Reggie did some quick calculating and determined that they were probably headed back to the warehouse where they were at the time of her discovery. Whatever business they were up to at the time must have still been waiting for their attention. She smiled inwardly, knowing Sheriff Ed Quinn would be an unexpected guest they'd soon have to deal with. Shifting her attention to Corbin, she lashed out. "Do you know what this is called? It's called kidnapping! Do you know what the penalty for kidnapping is?"

Corbin held up a hand. "Please, Regina, calm yourself. You were trespassing on my property. My men did only what they're paid to do when they encounter a trespasser. I assure you, you're in no danger. All I want is the chance to speak with you. There's a house just up the way. One of my employees, Amos Shepard, lives there. I noticed Amos fishing on the opposite side of the island when I came up in my boat. He won't mind if I use his place, and we can talk more comfortably there." Corbin took a step in the direction of the house, and Reggie was left with little choice but to follow him. At the moment she was at Corbin's mercy, but she was certain that would change in the near future. The tracking device was still in her purse, and she was positive Derrick would find a way to send help.

The house was the same one Reggie and Corbin had seen from the air when they flew over the island. "Who is this Amos Shepard?" she asked as they walked.

"Just a guy," Corbin said, obviously not willing to share any more information than he had already given. It was only a short walk to the house, and when they arrived, Corbin opened the door and led the way to a living room, where he offered Reggie a chair. "Let me check the refrigerator to see what Amos has to drink," Corbin said, stepping the short distance into the kitchen.

Reggie took this opportunity to check the place out. It was immaculate, and the furniture was arranged quite neatly. There was an overstuffed sofa with a coffee table in front of it, two recliners, a television set, three lamps at strategic locations throughout the room, and a well-stocked bookcase on one wall. There was also a fireplace with a painting of a lovely woman over the mantle. All signs indicated this was a well-kept and definitely lived-in home.

Corbin was back in a matter of seconds carrying two glasses of lemonade. "Please, sit," he said, offering her a glass. "Let's talk."

Reggie didn't trust Corbin, but for now she went along with him, as there were few other options. She took the lemonade and sat in one of the recliners while Corbin grabbed the other. "All right," she asked, "what's on your mind?"

"The same thing that was on my mind the first time we met," Corbin explained. "My brother. It seems he's doing his best to open some doors I want left closed. It's not my fault our father didn't leave him a shred of property, but that's the way it is. I have an uncontested will with our father's own signature to prove it. I asked you once for your help in discouraging Derrick's further interference. Now I find you snooping even deeper into my private life. I have no idea how you learned about the property in the desert, but you had no right breaking into it. The way I see it, I now have solid legal grounds to bring charges against you, Regina. But I'm willing to make you an even better offer than I did before. I hope you're smart enough to take my offer. After all, it's a win-win situation if you do, and a lose-lose situation if you don't."

Reggie was laughing inside since she knew the will Corbin was so proud of was anything but authentic. "You still want me to discourage Derrick from pursuing the mystery of your father's disappearance. Is that it, Corbin?" she asked.

Corbin leaned forward on the recliner. "You're Derrick's partner and his friend. He'll listen to you, Regina. I'm still willing to make it worth your while if you help me out here. And bear in mind, Derrick can't win even if he takes it to court."

Reggie laughed out loud. "First you kidnapped me and accuse me of trespassing in an attempt to whitewash it. Now you're offering me a bribe? I'm surprised, Corbin. These aren't the actions of a man who's certain of his position. You're on shaky ground, aren't you?"

Corbin's face turned ash gray. "I did not offer a bribe," he insisted. "What I'm offering is similar to a courtroom plea bargain. I don't need the publicity of a messy day in court, regardless of the fact that I can't lose."

Reggie laughed again. "This coming from the lips of the one who ordered my Firebird shot up? We'll talk about messy publicity when that gets out."

Corbin leaned back and set his glass down. "I'm guilty of a bad mistake there, and I'm the first to admit it. I'll take full responsibility for replacing the car with an even better one."

Reggie pressed her luck. "You're worried about Derrick opening an investigation into your father's disappearance because you have something to hide, don't you? You know what happened to your father, and I'm betting you were involved in whatever it was."

Corbin wet his lips and shifted his weight restlessly. "You're out of line, Regina. I've done nothing wrong."

"I think you have," she pressed. "And between your brother and me, we're going to prove it. You're obviously shaking in your boots right about now, Corbin, and well, you should be. You're going down. I know it, Derrick knows it, and you know it. Now if you don't mind, I'd like to borrow a phone to call for a ride out of here. Your accomplice stole mine when he kidnapped me."

* * *

Once Derrick satisfied himself that Reggie had probably been dropped off at the resort, he turned his attention back to Herb. "What's the story behind those buildings we just left? Were they built for the sole purpose of hiding the biplane, or were they built to hide something more? Like my father, for instance."

"You know this isn't easy for me, don't you, Derrick?"

"I don't care how easy it is for you, Herb! I want some answers, and I want them now!"

Derrick heard Herb exhale loudly into his mike. "Your father never got completely well, but he didn't die either," Herb explained with obvious difficulty. "Corbin wanted him taken care of, but he couldn't take the chance someone might stumble onto him and learn the truth. Your guess is right. Corbin did have the house at the desert facility built to hide Samuel. He referred to the place as 'the other property' and kept it hidden from everyone but Pepperton and me."

"Dad lived in that smaller building?" Derrick guessed.

"He lived there for about a year and a half," Herb admitted. "Doc Pepperton kept a close eye on him, and I talked Corbin into building the warehouse as a place to keep the biplane hidden. Once I had a permanent home for the plane, I had it reassembled and restored to its original condition."

Derrick's attention was suddenly drawn to another aircraft just coming into view ahead of them. *It's the chopper I saw take off with Reggie on board,* he quickly realized. *They must have dropped her off, and now they're headed back to the desert facility.* He was sure they hadn't spotted him, since he was flying on the edge of a cloud bank that made the small plane hard to see. He quickly maneuvered the craft further into the layer of clouds.

"What are you doing?" Herb cried, obviously frightened when he found himself inside a fog so thick he couldn't see as far as the end of the wing.

"Not to worry," Derrick responded. "I'm skilled at instrument flight. You're in no danger. I just caught sight of the chopper coming toward us, and I didn't want them to see us."

"Those guys work for Corbin, and the one called Ramsey is a dangerous man. Best to stay as far away from him as possible."

"Why do you think they're headed back to the warehouse, Herb?"

"They're after this plane, Derrick. They have orders to dismantle it and dump it in the ocean. Won't they be surprised to get there and find it gone?"

"Do you know how to use the radio in this thing?" Derrick asked.

"I do."

"Do you know who Sheriff Quinn is?"

"Yes, I know him."

"See if you can get a message to him. I'm a little busy flying this thing and trying to track Reggie's exact location. Tell Quinn those guys are in the chopper and where they're headed. Quinn already has a fix on the place. Tell him he can arrest those guys for shooting up my Cessna."

"Consider it done, Derrick. You keep us in the air, and I'll handle the radio."

As soon as Derrick felt it was safe, he dropped down again out of the clouds. To his relief, there was no sign of the chopper. He could only hope the trap would work. Glancing ahead, he noticed the resort just coming into sight. He checked the tracking device. It pointed to the island, of all places. "Why would they take Reggie to that island, Herb?" he asked.

"They took her to the island?" Herb countered in surprise. "The only reason I can think of is that Corbin feels safer there without the crowds at the resort. Can you land this thing on the island, Derrick?"

"Yeah, but hang on tight. It'll be a little rougher landing than usual."

CHAPTER 20

Amos reeled in his line and checked his bait. Nothing had bothered it, and he figured the fish just weren't biting today. Amos always liked to do his fishing on this side of the island, as far away from his house as possible. Not that the fishing was any better here. He just liked getting as far away from the house as he could since he had to spend so much time there anyway. He had noticed the resort chopper land somewhere near the boat dock, then take off again, and he had wondered what it was all about. But knowing Corbin the way he did, the chopper might have been there for any one of a hundred reasons.

Amos put a fresh worm on his hook and cast his line out to his favorite spot. Placing a few rocks against the rod to support it, he leaned back against the bank and stared up at the afternoon sky, where he spotted a couple of desert hawks gliding on the wind. Something about the birds triggered a feeling of freedom in Amos, sort of like he was the one up there gliding through those billowing clouds. This was even stronger than a feeling, though. This was like a glimmer of light trying fervently to penetrate the darkness hiding some cherished secret from his past. It was uncanny how these feeling occurred so strongly at times that they almost left him feeling like he was standing in front of a door marked *Yesterday*, a door that could almost be opened for a peek at the other side. Almost, but never quite. Amos sighed and tried to put such thoughts out of his mind.

Suddenly, something caught his eye. It was an airplane. He shaded his eyes with one hand and strained for a better look. "What do you know about that?" he said excitedly. "It's a beautiful old biplane. What would it be like, up there flying in one of those things?"

Amos's eyes remained glued to the plane as it drew closer. "That fella's going to fly right over the island," he muttered. "And he looks to be dropping down lower. Hot dog! A little excitement in my life. I get to watch a thing of beauty fly by me so close I can almost reach out and touch it."

Amos stood and stared in disbelief as he realized the pilot's intention seemed to be more than just a near pass to the island. He seemed to be intent on landing the thing. Amos knew of a strip of beach not far away where a little plane like that might set down, but to have one actually do it? "Now that would be something to write home about," Amos murmured to himself. "If a fellow had a home to write to, that is."

* * *

"Hang on, Herb!" Derrick yelled into the microphone. "We're going in!"

"Are you sure this is safe?" Herb replied, the hint of a tremor in his voice.

"I was with Dad once when he landed here, Herb. There's plenty of room to put this little baby down, and the sand is packed hard enough to support it."

Derrick had spotted a boat at the dock and assumed Reggie would be somewhere nearby, but landing on that side of the island would not only be impossible, it would be unwise. By landing on the other side, unseen, he could slip up on Reggie's captor without being noticed.

Just as he had warned Herb, the landing was a little rough, but he managed it perfectly. Taxiing the plane to a point he felt would be safe, he killed the engine, grabbed the tracking device reader, and hit the ground.

"You want me to come with you?" Herb called down from the cockpit.

"No. You stay here with the plane, where you have radio contact with Quinn. I feel a lot more comfortable with him knowing where we are, just in case."

Herb nodded. "You be careful, Derrick! And don't turn your back on Corbin!"

"That's something I learned a long time ago, Herb." Derrick turned and rushed into the thicket, all the while keeping a close check on the signal from the tracking device.

CHAPTER 21

Reggie found it disgusting that this man actually thought he might entice her into the kind of proposal he was suggesting. Was he really that naive? Or was he just used to being one who could bully his way through any situation? "I asked to borrow a phone," she reiterated, setting her drink aside and rising to her feet. "I assume there's one someplace in this house."

Corbin also stood. "I beg you to rethink your position, Regina," he pleaded. "You're making a big mistake if you think Derrick can stand up against me in court or anywhere else. Derrick is a loser. Always has been and always will be."

"A phone, Corbin!" Reggie coolly stated again. "We have nothing more to discuss, and I'd like to call for a ride home."

Corbin brushed a hand nervously through his hair. "There are no phones on this island," he stated.

No phones? Reggie thought. *How strange.* "Why no phones? Is there some reason Amos Shepard can't be trusted with one?"

"Never mind Amos Shepard!" Corbin bluntly retorted. "Amos is just someone who works for me. That's all you need to know."

Reggie couldn't help but notice the change creeping into Corbin's demeanor as she shifted her role in the conversation from the defensive to the offensive. He seemed unaccustomed to this and was allowing anger to noticeably lessen his stance as a man in complete charge. She remembered how he had reacted the first time they met, actually sending gunmen to shoot up her car after she withstood his barrage of demands. "Well now," she said, not backing off in the least, "it seems I've stumbled upon a touchy subject. There's something about Amos Shepard you don't want me to know, isn't there?"

"That's enough!" Corbin shouted. "You're out of line, Regina! No more talk about Amos Shepard!"

"All right," she politely agreed. "No more talk about Amos. But just so you know, I think a search warrant is in order for this island. I suspect when a judge hears how I was abducted and bribed, I won't have the slightest problem getting one. What do you think, Corbin?"

"No!" he barked. "I can't let you do that! I won't let you!"

"How do you plan on stopping me?" she pressed.

Reggie expected to strike a nerve with this little tactic, but she had no idea how much of a nerve. Suddenly a small firearm appeared in Corbin's hand. She suspected it had come from his back pocket. While Reggie may have misjudged the man, she certainly would never have guessed he might pull something as stupid as this.

"A gun?" she calmly asked. "You're adding assault to your list of growing charges? Not too bright, Corbin. Put the gun away and let me use the cell phone I know you have in your pocket."

Corbin's hand was shaking noticeably. Reggie was certain he wasn't used to pointing guns at people. "Why won't you listen to me?" he half shouted. "Why do you insist on pressing forward with an investigation that can't do anything but cause trouble? You'll gain nothing from it other than blackening my name. Is that what you want? To blacken my name?"

In the heat of their conversation, neither had noticed when Derrick eased his way into the room. When he spoke, all eyes centered on him. "Your name is already blackened, Corbin. You managed that on your own a very long time ago."

"Derrick!" Corbin bellowed. "How did you get here?"

"I was wondering that myself," Reggie broke in. "Although I have to admit, I am glad to see you. Even if you did take your sweet time showing up."

Corbin pointed the gun at Derrick. "Stay back!" he demanded. "I will use this if I have to!"

Derrick appeared unshaken. "You asked how I got here, Corbin. I'm sure you know it wasn't in a Cessna, since you had your dupes shoot out my tires. But that's okay. Tires can be fixed."

Corbin looked confused. "I didn't order anyone to . . ." His eyes suddenly widened. "Wait a minute! You were at the other property with Regina, weren't you?"

Derrick shook his head in disbelief. "Are you really that naive not to realize the presence of a Cessna at your property meant I'd be somewhere close by?"

"I should have known!" Corbin fumed. "But I don't know anything about your tires being shot. It must have been Ramsey's doing."

"Be that as it may, brother of mine. With the Cessna out of service, what other transportation would you suppose I might have found at that facility? Specifically in the warehouse?"

"I'd like to know that too," Reggie broke in.

"The biplane?" Corbin nervously surmised. "You found it!"

"That's it!" Reggie gasped. "You found your father's plane. It was hidden somewhere in that warehouse, wasn't it?" Without waiting for an answer, she added, "What about your dad? Did you find him too?"

Derrick shook his head. "I found the plane, but not Dad. I did find someone who knows Dad's fate, though. I just haven't dragged it out of him yet."

"Herb," Corbin growled through clenched teeth. "When I'm finished with him, he'll wish he'd never been born."

Derrick smiled. "I don't think so, brother. If anyone wishes they'd never been born before this is over, it'll probably be you."

"Not this time!" Corbin countered, the words rolling venomously off his tongue. "This time I'll be the one with the final laugh. You and your holier-than-thou attitude—always looking down on me like I'm nothing. Do these clothes I'm wearing look like nothing to you? This shirt alone cost more than you make in a week."

Derrick moved forward a few steps, quickly cutting the distance between him and Corbin in half. "The cost of a shirt? Is that what's important to you, Corbin? How about the way you've dealt with those who've reached out to touch you over the years? Shouldn't that say more about your true character than the cost of a shirt? Take the case of Vivian Lane. What does *that* say about the real you? Or the case of your own mother. She died with a broken heart, Corbin. And we both know who caused that broken heart, don't we?"

"Don't lay those things at my feet! Put the blame where it really belongs! On that church you're so in love with!"

"Nothing's ever your fault, is it, Corbin? Not on the surface anyway. But I can't help wondering how well you sleep at night. Is Vivian's ghost there to haunt you when the lights go out? And how about Mom? Does she—"

"Stop it!" Corbin exploded, cutting Derrick off in mid-sentence. "You may think you're my judge, but you're not!"

Derrick slowly inched the rest of the way to where Corbin was standing. "Give me the gun," he calmly stated.

Corbin's eyes anxiously shifted between the gun and Derrick's outstretched hand. His brow broke out in a cold sweat. "Give me the gun," Derrick firmly repeated. "We both know you're not going to use it. You never fired a gun in your life."

Something told Reggie that Derrick was right. Corbin wasn't the sort to use a gun. She wondered why he even had one with him now and could only conclude it had to do with him losing control as he watched his empire being threatened. As she looked on, Derrick simply reached out and took the gun from

Corbin's unprotesting hand. Derrick then ejected the clip and studied it closely. "This gun isn't even loaded," he stated. "What did you hope to accomplish with an unloaded gun, Corbin?"

"I hate you," Corbin whispered as Derrick tossed the gun and clip on the sofa. "And if you think I'm going to stand by and let you take away what's rightfully mine—"

"Tell me, Corbin," Derrick interrupted. "Why did you have this house built? And more pointedly, who lives here?"

"Nothing about this resort is any of your business! I don't owe you explanations about this house or anything else. And I won't tolerate you and your girlfriend snooping around in my affairs anymore. I don't want a court battle, but if you insist on interfering where you don't belong, I will come down on you hard. Are you listening to me, Derrick?"

"I can answer your question about the house," Reggie spoke up. "The man who lives here is named Amos Shepard. And it seems your brother has a few secrets about Amos he wants kept that way."

"Amos Shepard, eh?" Derrick pondered. "Answer me this, Corbin. Why would Amos Shepard hang a painting of our mother over the fireplace?"

Reggie glanced quickly at the painting. "That's your mother?" she gasped.

"It's not only a portrait of our mother," Derrick disclosed. "It's one painted by our own father. I'd recognize his work anywhere. This one I haven't seen before, Corbin. Which brings up an interesting question. When exactly did Dad paint it?"

Corbin's eyes narrowed and his jawline tightened, but for the moment he remained mute.

"You know what I think, brother? I think you know a lot more about our father's fate than you're letting on. Would you like to fill me in on what you know, or would you rather I dig it out on my own? And rest assured, I will dig it out. Every dirty piece of it!"

"Enough of this! I don't care what it takes, I want you out of my life once and for all!"

Suddenly the attention of everyone in the room was captured by the unexpected sound of an airplane. Derrick was the first to realize what it was. "The biplane!" he shouted. "Someone's flying it off the island!"

In three bounds, Derrick was out the door with Reggie and Corbin right on his heels. Reggie's heart leapt as she glanced at the sky to see the little yellow biplane climbing majestically over the tops of the trees into the afternoon sky. "How can this be?" Derrick gasped. "I left Herb in charge of the plane, but he can't fly it!" Once the plane reached a few hundred feet, it slowly banked in a direction headed for Phoenix.

"No!" Corbin shouted. "Not this!"

For a very long moment, Derrick just stood watching the plane shrink into the distant horizon. At last he spoke what his mind had gradually conceived. "There's only one man who could be at those controls, and we both know who it is, don't we, Corbin?"

Corbin slumped onto a large rock, where he buried his face in his hands. "This can't be happening," he moaned.

"I want some answers, Corbin!" Derrick demanded. "What is going on here?"

"Look!" Reggie cried, catching sight of a motorboat speeding their way. "We're about to have company." A smile crossed her lips as the boat came near enough for her to recognize the driver as Ed Quinn. He must have impounded the boat from the resort to come after them. "All right!" she exclaimed. "Score a point for the good guys!"

"Is everything under control here?" Quinn yelled as he cut the engine, allowing the boat to coast up to the dock.

"Yes!" Reggie called back. "Everything's completely under control now. But we sure could use a ride off this island."

"It looks like Herb stayed busy on the radio," Derrick

remarked. "He must have guided Quinn straight to us." Derrick turned to stare down at Corbin again. "I'm not exactly sure what you've been up to here, Corbin, but whatever it is, time's just run out. You may not be willing to furnish answers, but I'll find those answers with or without you." Corbin didn't even look up. "Not much comfort from those expensive clothes you're wearing about now, is there?" Derrick continued. "From my viewpoint, I'd say your world as you know it is about to come crashing down. It makes me wonder. How will you go about blaming the Church this time?"

* * *

Long after the boat taking Derrick and Reggie off the island disappeared, Corbin remained seated on the rock. At last he reached down and scooped up a handful of sand, which he allowed to sift through his fingers until it had all fallen back to the earth. Was this a foreshadowing of what was to become of his empire?

Corbin stood and glanced back at the house. "How many times have you been a thorn in my side, Derrick?" he muttered to himself. "And now you return to extract another pound of flesh! But why should I worry? I have a legal document backing me up, one with Father's signature on it. And it was signed before he lost command of his faculties. You may have set me back, but you won't win this one, Derrick! What's mine is mine, and it will remain mine!"

Corbin returned to the house with the intention of closing the door that had been left open in the commotion. Once there, something compelled him to go inside to the painting of his mother hanging over the fireplace. There he stood, gazing into her eyes for a full minute or more. "I miss you," he finally said. "I miss you more than you can possibly know. I love Father. I've always loved him. But not the same way I loved you. You were the only one who ever understood me. How I wish you were here now to help me know what to do."

Corbin's eyes lowered as he realized what he had just said. Did he really wish his mother were here to tell him what to do when he knew perfectly well what her counsel would be?

Suddenly angry at himself for his moment of weakness, Corbin turned and hurried out of the house, slamming the door behind him. If it was a fight Derrick wanted, then it was a fight Derrick would have.

* * *

"All right, Quinn!" Derrick exclaimed once the boat was on the lake and speeding toward the mainland. "Tell me how you managed to get here so fast! You'd barely be clearing the Mesa city limit sign right now if you had abided by our agreement."

Quinn laughed. "I cheated, son. Did you really think I was going to let you and Reggie go snooping around those facilities with me still in the valley?"

"And you didn't bother explaining you were already on the job when Herb contacted you from the biplane?"

"I was too busy at the moment for explanations, Derrick. I had an investigation to run. It seems a certain Cessna had two flattened tires, there was a possible kidnapping, and a couple of aircrafts had mysteriously taken off from the place before I got there."

"Well, I for one am glad you cheated," Reggie cut in. "I was getting tired of that island, and I'm darned glad for a ride home."

"You'll also be glad to know that my boys arrested the two dimwits who grabbed you, Regg. I'm positive they'll turn out to be the ones who shot up your car. And get this—when my guys ran background checks, it seems that the one named Ramsey Borden had a warrant out on him for shooting some guy in Denver just two days ago."

Reggie laughed. "That doesn't surprise me. Borden's a real work of art. Where'd you arrest them? Back at the facilities where they nabbed me?"

"Yeah. I worked a deal with Clint to leave a couple of my officers guarding the Cessna until he could get a crew of mechanics out to rescue it. Had 'em keep their car in the warehouse and stay out of sight just in case something should happen like those guys coming back. Caught 'em red-handed when they set their chopper down."

"That's all well and good," Derrick remarked, "but I want to know about a certain pilot that just flew a yellow biplane out of here."

"I'll just bet you do," Quinn laughed. "I have it on good authority that the pilot you're talking about will be transported straight to Desert Samaritan Hospital as soon as the little yellow plane touches down at Falcon Field. The police chopper is on its way here to pick us up now. I could probably be persuaded to have them drop you off at Desert Sam on our way back. Who knows? Maybe someone there can answer your questions better than this tired old sheriff."

CHAPTER 22

Being flown to a hospital in a police chopper was a first for Reggie, but she was glad the experience came under these circumstances and not because she was being rushed there for her own medical attention. Sheriff Quinn wanted to remain at the hospital with them, but urgent police business dictated otherwise, so he left with the chopper crew. An orderly identifying himself as Mel Casey met them at the chopper pad. "We may have a difficult time getting past all the reporters," Casey explained as the chopper pulled away. "We have a hospital full of 'em."

"Reporters?" Reggie quizzed.

Casey laughed. "I take it you haven't seen the evening news, or you wouldn't seem so surprised. When a legend like Samuel Beatty suddenly drops out of the sky after being in outer space for the past five years, it's bound to cause some buzzing of the news bees."

"Then it's true!" Derrick exclaimed. "It really was Dad flying the plane?"

"Yep. Flew his famous plane right into Falcon Field not two hours ago. They transported him and his old mining partner, Herb Solomon, here to Desert Sam right away. Been doing tests on him ever since." Casey paused for a closer look at Derrick. "So you're Samuel's son? I'll bet you've got a case of the nerves waiting to see the old man again."

"I've been more nervous, but I can't remember when. So do I get to see him or what?"

"Just as soon as they get through poking him full of needles and taking pictures of his insides. Come on with me, I'll take you to a private room where you can wait without all the hassle of those reporters. I suggest you don't identify yourself if any of 'em catch you on the way."

To Reggie's relief, they made it past the reporters just fine, thanks in a big part to Mel Casey's knowledge of all the back routes through the hospital. After Casey got them settled in a private room, he had a couple of soft drinks sent in. Derrick flipped on the television to find every channel blaring the news of Samuel's sudden return from the dead. Every reporter had a different speculation as to where Samuel had been the past five years and what circumstances had brought him home now. Derrick soon tired of it and shut it off.

Reggie watched as he paced nervously from one end of the room to the other and back again, yet even the worry in his eyes couldn't distract from his handsomeness. Reggie could only imagine what he must have been feeling, and her heart yearned for a way to comfort him. It seemed like an eternity before two men stepped through the door. One was obviously a doctor, and the other was Herb Solomon. Reggie had never met Herb, but she recognized him immediately from old news clips.

"I'm Dr. Walker," the one said, offering his hand to Derrick, who had crossed the small room to meet him halfway. "You're Derrick Beatty, I assume?"

"I'm Derrick, yes! Have you seen my father?"

"Been with him the past hour and a half. Quite a colorful man, I must say."

"Is he—all right? When can I see him?"

The doctor laughed. "I understand how anxious you must be. Your father's getting dressed now. They'll draw some blood, then they'll bring him down." The doctor turned to Reggie. "You must be Mrs. Beatty?"

Reggie coughed. "No, no! I'm Derrick's partner. We're private detectives."

"Oh, I'm sorry. Bad assumption on my part."

"No harm done," she said, wishing her heart would slow back to its normal pace.

"What can you tell me about my dad, Doctor? Is he all right?"

The doctor put his arm around Derrick's shoulders. "Your father's going to be fine. I'm not saying he doesn't have some problems to overcome, but nothing life threatening. Maybe we should let Herb here fill you in, since he pretty much knows the whole story. I'll fill in the medical jargon as necessary."

Herb cleared his throat, then, looking at Reggie, he asked, "Has Derrick filled you in on what I've told him already about the explosion and all?"

"Yes, Herb. He told me on the way here to the hospital."

"Good. Then I won't have to go over that part again."

"Herb!" Derrick pleaded. "Will you get on with it! I think I've waited long enough!"

"Well, I told you that no one expected Samuel to live, but he fooled us all. He was tougher than any of us gave him credit for. But he didn't come through it without setbacks. When he came out of the coma, his memory was pretty much gone."

"Dad lost his memory?" Derrick gasped. "All of it?"

"Pretty much, Derrick. He retained a few things, like his ability to paint and his religious beliefs, but nothing from his past life. Not even his own name. The specialists at the California hospital worked with him long and hard, but in the end they theorized he'd probably never have the bulk of his memory back. We were told some victims with similar problems had been known to recover at least a partial memory, but even this was rare. They suggested we surround Samuel with familiar things and places, as this would be the best shot at him getting anything back at all."

"Wait a minute," Derrick broke in. "If I understand it right, Dad was first kept in the house next to where the biplane was hidden, then moved to the island and told he was Amos Shepard. This doesn't sound like familiar surroundings. Corbin didn't want Dad's memory coming back, did he?"

Herb shifted his weight nervously. "I know I should have had the guts to stand up to your brother, but I needed the money he was paying me to keep my mouth shut just to stay alive. I was indebted to those gambling lords from Las Vegas, and they play for keeps."

"So Corbin invented Amos Shepard and saw to it Dad was fed enough information to actually believe that's who he was? One thing I don't get is how Corbin kept Dad on that island and out of sight from the world."

"He did it with more lies," Herb explained. "Once Corbin had your dad believing he was Amos Shepard, he convinced him a warrant was out for his arrest on charges of murdering the real Samuel Beatty."

"What!" Derrick shouted. "Corbin convinced Dad he killed . . . himself?"

"Well, sort of. He did it by inventing a fake past for Samuel Beatty. Corbin took my gambling problem and shifted it to his made-up Samuel. From there, the story gets complicated."

Derrick brushed a hand through his hair. "It gets complicated from there? I'd say it's already reached the complicated stage."

Reggie, who had been quietly listening to Herb's story, spoke up. "Let me interject a theory here," she proposed. "Samuel Beatty was supposedly in deep with the gambling lords from Las Vegas. Amos Shepard was supposedly a hit man working for those gambling lords." The look in Herb's eye told Reggie she was close to the mark with her proposed story. She went on. "Amos was led to believe he enticed Samuel into the old mine, where he had prestaged an explosion with the intention of making it appear as an accident. Only something went wrong, and Amos ended up in the middle of the explosion himself. How close am I Herb?"

"Darn close," Herb acknowledged. "Except Amos was supposedly a cop who was trying to save Samuel's life. Another fictitious hit man was supposed to have set off the explosion. Corbin got Amos believing he had actually tried to stop the killing, but ended up nearly getting himself killed in the act. The rest of the concocted story had circumstantial evidence pointing to Amos as the real killer. Corbin came across as the good guy who wanted to protect Amos from an almost certain fate of spending the rest of his life in prison."

"All right," Derrick stated, "next question. If Dad thinks he's Amos Shepard—a wanted man—why did he fly the plane back to Mesa?"

"That's the fantastic part, Derrick! After you landed the plane on the island and went to look for Reggie, Amos—that is, Samuel—showed up. Something about that old plane triggered his memory. He remembered it!"

"Dad remembered his plane? That makes sense. I think he loved that old plane almost as much as he loved me."

"But that's not all. Once he remembered the plane, a few more things came back. He remembered me, Derrick. As his old partner, I mean. Then, with my help, he figured out his name was really Samuel Beatty, not Amos Shepard. I know you Mormons are always talking about miracles, and well, I think I watched one happen right there on the spot. That's when I contacted Quinn and told him everything that was going on. I asked what I should do, and Quinn told me to stay put until he could get the police chopper to us. Samuel wanted no part of it. He agreed that he wanted off the island, but he wanted to fly himself out. Once he remembered where Falcon Field was located, there was no stopping him. It was just like old times.

The real Samuel Beatty was back. I figured I'd better tag along just in case. Buzzing the house was my idea. It was the only way I had of letting you know something was up."

"Thanks for that, Herb. It was a shock, but a good one."

"When Samuel identified himself to the airport tower, the whole world went nuts. By the time he got the plane on the ground, every news reporter in Arizona had gotten wind of what was happening. If Quinn hadn't radioed ahead and had a car waiting for us, we'd probably still be trying to fight our way out of a reporter nightmare. We were out of that airport in less time than it takes an egg to boil."

"Your father's in amazingly good health," Dr. Walker broke in. "And he's remembered even more since the initial things Herb's mentioned. He knows who you are, and now he knows the truth about your brother. But I don't want to get your hopes up too high. It's very unlikely his memory will ever completely return. Just be thankful for what he has."

"Dad kept a detailed journal from the time he was thirteen," Derrick excitedly announced. "Even if he can't remember everything, he can at least know himself from his own words."

"Excellent," Dr. Walker remarked. "A reconstructed memory to take the place of the one lost. Yes, I'd say that is worth something."

Reggie was the first to see him at the door, as the others had their backs turned. He looked slightly older than the Samuel Beatty she remembered, and he had one large scar running diagonally down from his hairline to just over his right eye, but it was him! Tears gushed from her eyes as they met his. She knew right away he didn't remember her, but that was okay. Very slowly, she stepped to Derrick, took ahold of his shoulders, and turned him around to face his father. "Hello, son," came the most beautiful voice Reggie could remember hearing. "Who's the lovely young woman? Have you gone and gotten yourself married since the last time I saw you?"

CHAPTER 23

A wave of nausea settled in the pit of Corbin's stomach as he stared at the four gray walls surrounding him. The same four gray walls of the same cold cell he'd been looking at for the past three months. This was disgusting, and someone was going to pay big-time for forcing him to endure this humiliation. What a stroke of ill-fated luck it had been when a judge was convinced to freeze the assets for Beatty Enterprises until everything could be settled in court. With the assets frozen, Corbin could no longer afford the team of lawyers he was accustomed to having at his command. What he ended up with was a fool appointed by the court who didn't have enough savvy to blow his own nose, let alone convince a judge to set bail at a reasonable amount. As it was, Corbin still had two weeks of this stinking place to endure before the trial date. He could only hope this miserable excuse for a lawyer wouldn't be clumsy enough to blow a court case with the ton of concrete evidence Corbin had behind him.

None of this would ever have happened if that meddling Derrick hadn't returned home to stick his nose in where it didn't belong. And how could those specialists from California have been so wrong about Samuel's memory being lost forever? Corbin had no idea how much memory his father had recovered, as he hadn't heard a thing from him or Derrick since being incarcerated. Corbin was positive Samuel couldn't have remembered much—just as he was sure the whole bunch of them would be crying what a miracle it was that he got anything back at all. Mormons always cried "Miracle!" at times like this. It disgusted Corbin just thinking about what they must have been saying.

Truth be known, this was anything but a miracle. Corbin had been taking excellent care of his father the way things were, and he would have cared for him for the rest of his life. In spite of what anyone might have thought, Corbin loved his father and wanted only the best for him. After the accident, the best thing was the life Corbin had provided on the little island. Samuel had every comfort he needed—Corbin had seen to that. Not that anyone would ever give him credit now that the world had gotten a look inside his personal affairs. Now Corbin would be made to look like nothing more than an unloving son who forced his own will on his father. Corbin grabbed his pillow and flung it against the far wall. "How can this be happening?" he moaned. "It just isn't fair."

Corbin let his eyes move upward from the pillow to the painting of his mother that hung on the otherwise bare wall above it. It was the same painting that had hung in Amos Shepard's house on the little island for such a long time. Corbin's appointed lawyer hadn't been good for much else, but he had managed to convey Corbin's wish for the painting in his cell in a manner that those in charge concurred with. At times, especially in the evenings, the painting made Corbin feel like his mother was really there with him. In a way this was wonderful, yet in another way it was frightening. More and more, again especially in the evenings, feelings of remorse had begun creeping in at the realization he had lived a failed life. This was a realization he didn't want to think about, but one that refused to remain outside the boundaries of his mind as he looked into his mother's tender eyes. As a result, Corbin was left with a bit of a war waging inside himself, a war being fought between the man he was and the man he couldn't help but feel his mother had wished he might be. He did his best to keep these things clear of his mind, and he certainly couldn't admit his conflict to another living soul. If the Mormons heard of it, they'd swear it was because someone was praying for him.

At that moment, a guard stepped up to his cell. "Ya got a visitor, Beatty," he said, unlocking the cell door. "And is she ever a looker. On yer feet, pal."

Corbin stood and stared at the guard. "A visitor? Who?" It was a question worth asking since in the three months he had been here not one visitor had shown up—unless you counted that fool of a lawyer. But the guard had indicated this visitor was a woman. "Well, ya just gunna stand there starin'?" the guard snorted.

Corbin ran a hand over the stubble of beard on his face. There was nothing he could do about the way he looked now. He stepped through the gate and listened to the nauseating sound of the latch clicking shut behind him, a sound he had developed a staunch hatred for in the last three months. Though Corbin had never had a visitor of his own, he had talked to some of the other inmates who described the way it was normally done. The inmate would be led to a room where he was seated on a stool looking through a set of bars at his visitor. To Corbin's surprise, the room where he was taken wasn't like that at all. When the door to his meeting room opened, he looked inside to see that it looked more like a conference room. There was a table with two chairs, and the visitor the guard had described was standing near one of the chairs. The guard was right about her being a looker. She was dressed in a finely styled business suit.

"This is Counselor Dalton," the guard explained. Then, addressing the woman, he said, "The phone on the desk is a direct line ta the guard station. When yer done, pick up the phone and pass the message along ta whoever answers. I'll be back ta pick Beatty up."

The guard closed the door, leaving Corbin and this woman, Counselor Dalton, alone. "Please," the counselor said, pointing to one of the chairs, "won't you be seated?"

Corbin obliged, and the woman took a seat across the table from him. "What's this all about?" Corbin asked suspiciously.

"It's about your future," the counselor answered. "I'm here on behalf of your father."

Corbin stiffened. "I thought the State Attorney's office was handling the prosecution. I know you're not one of them. Has my father hired you to put even more pressure on me?"

"No, actually your father is considering hiring me to represent you, Corbin. That is, if you're interested in pursuing your case in a manner I'm here to discuss with you."

Corbin's brow raised as he contemplated the meaning of this. "Dad wants to hire a lawyer to represent me?" he questioned. "There has to be a catch. What is it?"

The counselor smiled. "Let's talk, Corbin."

"All right," Corbin agreed. "We can talk. But just to set the stage, let me point out exactly where I stand on this matter. The prosecution has made a big thing about freezing my assets and putting me in this humiliating position. But the fact is, when we meet in a courtroom, I'm the one holding all the aces. I have a document legally signed by my father at a time when he was in command of his faculties, and that document places me in complete charge of Beatty Enterprises. After the noise of the drums is silenced, I'll be the last one standing. I'm the one most qualified to oversee my father's affairs in his present condition, and my decision is to return him to his place on the island where he can live out his days in peace and comfort."

The counselor opened her briefcase and removed two sets of papers. She handed one set to Corbin. "I'd like to have you look these over, if you will. These papers contain the results of medical and psychological testing your father has undergone since recovering his memory. You'll notice the evaluators have given him a clean bill of health. He's perfectly capable of handling his own affairs, Corbin."

Anger boiled in Corbin's mind. "That's preposterous!" he snapped. "I can have my own psychologists evaluate him, and I'm sure their findings will conflict with this bogus report. My father is most certainly *not* capable of making complex, intelligent decisions. Not with the injuries he sustained in that explosion."

"You're wrong, you know. You're father's quite a man, really. Whether you know it or not, Corbin, he loves you a great deal. Enough to make the effort to keep you out of prison."

"More absurdity! How can you threaten me with prison when I'm the one holding all the aces in this game?"

The counselor handed Corbin the second set of papers she had taken from her case. "Do you recognize this?" she asked.

One look was all it took for Corbin to realize what she had given him this time. "You're darn right I recognize this," he flatly stated. "It's Dad's will giving me sole ownership of Beatty Enterprises. You *have* read this will, haven't you?"

"Oh, I've read every word in it, Corbin. And I've taken a long, hard look at the signature on the bottom. Have you?"

More anger filled Corbin's mind as he contemplated what this woman was getting at. "Of course I've looked at it! It's my father's signature. What else is there to say about it?"

"Go back to the other documents, Corbin. The ones evaluating your father's health and mental well-being. I want you to compare Samuel's signature on those documents to the one on the will. The differences between the two are so drastic that even an untrained eye could readily tell they're from two separate people."

Corbin made a quick comparison of the two signatures. A jolt of hot fear shot up his spine as he realized her statement was right. "This can't be!" he gasped. "I know my father signed this will."

"Do you?" the counselor proposed. "Or are you taking the word of your Dr. Pepperton for that fact?"

Cold sweat instantly beaded on Corbin's brow. Had Pepperton lied to him? The old fool swore he had coerced

Samuel to apply his signature to the document. Corbin lifted his eyes to face the counselor again. "We've had handwriting experts examine the signature, Corbin. I think you can guess who we learned really signed the document. Can't you?"

"Doc Pepperton," Corbin guessed in a weakened voice that came out as barely more than a whisper.

The counselor nodded, then asked, "Are you ready to talk now?"

CHAPTER 24

The name *Judge Garret* was written in large, black letters on the heavy oak door. Reggie couldn't stifle her curiosity about the conversation she knew was taking place inside. Neither she nor Derrick had any idea what the conversation was about, but what they did know was that Samuel had employed a new lawyer to replace the one appointed by the court to represent both Corbin and Herb. This new lawyer had something going that had prompted her to set up this pretrial hearing with Judge Garret. The representative from the State Attorney's office was inside with the new lawyer, as was Samuel himself. Corbin, who had spent the preceding three months softening up in a jail cell, hadn't been brought in just yet.

Reggie stepped up to Derrick and adjusted the knot on his tie. "It's going to be all right," she consoled, realizing how nervous he was. "You're blowing things all out of proportion."

"Does it show that much?" Derrick asked, feigning a smile.

"Like stripes on a zebra. Why are you letting this bother you so? This time Corbin's out of bullets."

"I know that, Regg. But Dad's been through so much already, and regardless of how guilty Corbin may be, he's still Dad's son. What's it going to do to Dad to know that one of his sons will spend who knows how many years in state prison?"

"It's not just your dad you're concerned about, is it? You don't like the idea of seeing your brother end up in prison either, do you?"

Derrick blew out a long breath. "Corbin is still my brother," he admitted. "But I can't erase what he's done, and I can't keep him from paying the price."

Reggie's thoughts were interrupted when she spotted a uniformed officer escorting Corbin into the outer office where she and Derrick were waiting just outside the judge's chambers. "Guess who?" she whispered to Derrick.

Derrick sighed, and turned to look for himself. As Corbin drew near, he and Derrick stared at each other without speaking. Reggie reached for Derrick's hand and gave it a gentle squeeze. The awkwardness of the moment was mercifully shortened when the door to Judge Garret's chambers opened. "The judge is ready for the rest of you now," a man at the door announced.

Judge Garret stood as they entered the room. Reggie spotted the prosecution at a table on the left of the judge's desk. She did a double take when she spotted Samuel sitting at the table on the opposite side, next to Corbin's new lawyer. What was this all about?

Corbin was led to a chair next to his lawyer, where he sat down. Again, to Reggie's astonishment, she and Derrick were motioned to seats next to Samuel. This made no sense at all. Shouldn't they have been on the side of the prosecution? She and Derrick exchanged glances, and she knew he was just as confused by this arrangement as she was. They took their seats. The new attorney leaned over close to Corbin and whispered some words of instruction to him. After this was done, she stood and addressed the judge. "My client has been fully advised as to what's being considered here, Your Honor. He's in full accord. We're ready to proceed when you are."

Full accord for what? Reggie asked herself. *What is going on here?*

"Very well," the judge responded. "Let me explain some things. This is not a trial, but I expect everyone involved to take this proceeding as seriously as if it were a trial. You won't be under oath here, and nothing said in this meeting will be permissible as evidence in trial, if a trial becomes necessary. But I want it understood that if we can reach an agreement in this room that keeps this case from going to trial, it's this judge's opinion that it's a win-win situation all the way around." The judge turned to face the prosecution, whose head lawyer was a man introduced as Lloyd Fairchild. "Okay, Counselor Fairchild. The floor is yours."

Fairchild stood. "To bring everyone up-to-date, let me explain that the prosecution has agreed to drop all charges against Herb Solomon, on the condition that Herb receive counseling for his gambling problem and that he serve three hundred hours of community service. It seems even the victim, Mr. Samuel Beatty, agrees with this course. In fact, I'm told it was Mr. Beatty who initiated the idea."

Reggie glanced at Derrick, who was looking back at her. This was unexpected news, but good news as far as Reggie was concerned. She knew Derrick agreed. "The defense has proposed we take similar action in Corbin's case," Fairchild continued. "But we want to take a long, hard look at this one before coming to any decision. Corbin was guilty of a greater offense than Herb. If it pleases the court, I'd like to direct my preapproved instruction to Corbin at this time."

So that's what this was about? Reggie couldn't help the tear that slid down one cheek as she realized Samuel was willing to forgive his son and do everything in his power to keep Corbin from serving time in prison. It would take some real doing, she reasoned, to forgive a son who had done the things Corbin was guilty of. Reggie had already come to love this new Samuel, whom she had known slightly more than three months. This bit of knowledge about his character elevated him to even greater heights in her eyes. "We have no objections to this," Reggie heard the new attorney say.

"You may proceed," the judge instructed.

"Who is this attorney?" Derrick whispered to his father. "And is what she's up to agreeable with you?"

"Her name is Counselor Dalton," Samuel whispered back. "She actually approached me with the idea of what we're shooting for here. Just pay attention. I think you're going to like the way she works."

"Has your attorney explained what it is I want from you before we discuss a possible pretrial settlement, Mr. Beatty?"

* * *

Fairchild's words cut Corbin to the quick. Never in his life had he felt so totally defeated. Counselor Dalton had explained what the prosecution wanted in exchange for considering her proposals. They wanted to hear an apology. It had to be an apology from deep enough in his heart to convince the prosecution of his genuine remorse. Apologizing was something Corbin had never been good at, and therefore something he had seldom done. "Did you understand my question, Mr. Beatty?" Fairchild said again.

Corbin swallowed. "Yes, sir," he responded. "I understand."

"Well, then, what do you have to say for yourself?"

Corbin reached into his shirt pocket and removed a Polaroid photo he had talked one of the guards into snapping of his mother's painting. For a long, torturous moment, he stared into her eyes. *Help me, Mother,* he pleaded in his own heart. *I can't do this without you.*

Corbin could feel every eye in the room burning through him. Once again, he looked at the picture of his mother. "Father," he began, "no one told me exactly who it was I'm supposed to apologize to. I, uh, think I'd like to talk straight to you." As the sound of Corbin's words faded, the whole room went dead silent. Corbin drew a deep breath and forced himself to go on. "I was wrong in what I did. I honestly thought you would never regain any degree of your memory, but I was wrong to hide you from the world in order to further my own . . ." The words trickled off for another space of silence before Corbin picked up again. "In order to further my own greedy desires."

Corbin looked at the picture of his mother, and he could have sworn she was smiling more brightly than ever before. Then it hit him. These words he was uttering weren't so hard to say when it was actually his heart doing the speaking. He realized suddenly that it *was* his heart doing the speaking. A volcano of emotion erupted within him as he realized this was not some show of contrived remorse. For the first time, he realized the magnitude of what he had done—and he was sorry. Truly sorry. Shoving the chair aside, he stood and rounded the table to look his father straight in the eye. "I'm so sorry," he said. "And not just for what I did to you after your accident. I'm sorry I was never the son you deserved. I'm sorry for what I did to Mom."

Corbin's eyes squeezed closed as salty tears spilled from beneath the lids. There was so much more he wanted to say just now, but his voice faltered.

After a long speechless moment, Corbin heard Counselor Fairchild again address the judge. "I'm satisfied," he said. "Here's what we want. The defendant is to be gainfully employed within one month of his release, and he's to maintain gainful employment for a period of not less than three years. He's to personally reimburse my office for all costs incurred in this case. We also want him to perform one thousand hours of community service. I'll have this drawn up for signatures one week from today."

The judge turned to Corbin. "Is this agreeable?" she asked.

* * *

Reggie wasn't the only one in the room with dampened eyes by the time the sound of the judge's gavel marked the end of the hearing. Samuel didn't even try to cover his show of emotion, and Derrick did a poor job of covering his. He might have fooled some, but certainly not Reggie. She thought about teasing him, but decided this was too delicate a moment for that sort of thing. Once outside the chambers, a little group of uneasy people formed. A great deal had already been done to clear the air, but the friction was still apparent as Derrick and Corbin came together again. "That was some apology," Derrick managed to say, with only Reggie realizing how hard it was for him to do.

"Yeah," Corbin responded. "But I'm not sure it accomplished what it was intended to do. For me to stay out of prison, I have to find a job. Where am I going to find a job with the limited skills I've developed in my years of chasing one rainbow after another?"

"You were always good at woodwork," Derrick reminded him. "I still have that family crest you carved for me when we were in high school. I've kept it hanging on the wall of every office I've had since."

Corbin eyed his brother more closely. "You kept that thing?" he asked. "Why?"

"I don't know. It just reminded me of better days between us, I guess. And it's a pretty nice piece of work. You did a good job on it, Corbin."

Corbin forced a smile. "Thanks. Coming from you, that's a compliment."

Derrick cleared his throat. "Would you be interested in a job in furniture construction?" he asked. "I know a guy. I could put in a good word for you."

Reggie let her eyes shift back and forth between these two brothers. Was this really happening? Were they actually trying to get along? "I'd love a shot at furniture construction," Corbin quickly responded. "I mean, since I'm being forced to go back to work someplace."

Derrick actually laughed at this. "Going to be tough, eh? Too many years telling everyone else what to do at the resort?"

"Cut me a little slack, Derrick. This isn't easy, you know."

"I'll put in a good word with my friend. If all goes well, you can probably go to work Monday."

There was a moment when Reggie thought the two would actually manage a hug, but it never materialized. It didn't matter, though. A wedge had made its way into the closed door between them, allowing a ray of sunlight to pass through.

"Glad to see you two at least speaking," Counselor Dalton broke in. "You know what they call this in the Mormon Church, don't you, Corbin?"

Corbin rolled his eyes. "You're a Mormon? I should have guessed. I give up. What do they call it?"

"It's a new beginning." She smiled. "Something I'm a little familiar with myself."

"New beginning," Corbin echoed. "If I remember right, it had something to do with a girls' program."

"Well, in your case, Corbin, as well as in my own case, it had more to do with life itself. Let me ask you a question. Does the name *Vivian Lane* mean anything to either of you?"

Reggie caught her breath as she watched Derrick and Corbin exchange nervous glances. "I've heard the name, yes," Corbin admitted.

"I happen to know Vivian quite well," the counselor said. "I know the story of how she was in an accident with you, Corbin. And I know what happened to her from there."

"You do?" This time it was Derrick who spoke. "Can you tell us?"

Reggie wasn't sure if she liked the spark of hope in Derrick's voice. In all honesty, it did leave her feeling a little jealous of Vivian Lane if the woman could still draw out this side of Derrick.

"I assume you both know the story up to the point of Vivian's father giving up his practice here in Mesa and moving away. So, that's where I'll start. They moved to Seattle,

Washington. There were several reasons behind the move, but the foremost reason was a Dr. Fitzgerald, who came highly recommended in the skill of reconstructive surgery."

Corbin paled. "I saw her face, Counselor. I doubt there was a skilled enough surgeon alive who could have done much for her."

"Dr Fitzgerald was pretty good," the counselor refuted. "Vivian underwent seven surgeries altogether. She also attended counseling to help her emotional wounds heal. In time, she began putting the pieces back together. She even returned to college, pursuing her lifetime dream to follow in her father's footsteps."

"She wanted to be a lawyer," Derrick observed.

The counselor smiled and nodded. "That was probably her second biggest dream, after finding a husband who'd marry her in the temple," she explained. "To keep the story short, Vivian became a respected attorney in her father's firm. But she was never happy working under his shadow. Not that she didn't love and appreciate him and all he had done. It's just that she wanted to prove she could make it on her own. That's when she returned to Mesa."

"She what?" Corbin gasped. "Vivian came back to Mesa as an attorney?" After a moment's thought, he asked, "Is she still here?"

"Would it matter to you if she was here?"

Reggie saw a look of pain fill Corbin's eyes. "If I could erase one thing from my life, it would be what I did to that lovely woman. There's no way she deserved what happened to her. You may find this hard to believe, but I was in love with Vivian. Truth be known, I probably still am. I should have known from the start it wouldn't work between us. Not with my attitude about the church she loved. You ask if it would matter to me knowing she was here in Mesa. In all honesty, I probably wouldn't like knowing that at all. I wish Vivian all the happiness in the world, and that is the truth. I swear it on my mother's grave. But could I ever face her again? I'd sooner walk a mile barefoot over red-hot coals."

The counselor's smile widened. "Vivian not only attained her dream of becoming an attorney, she also attained her bigger dream of a temple marriage. She met a very handsome and successful doctor. They've been married a little over a year now."

"Vivian's married?" Corbin commented. "I—I'm glad." Gathering his courage, he ventured into a more difficult question. "Her face? How disfigured is it?"

At this, Counselor Dalton broke into light laughter. "Why not be the judge of that yourself?" she asked.

Reggie gasped as the foundation for this conversation struck home. "Dr. Fitzgerald did a good job, wouldn't you say?" the counselor asked. "It's not the face I was born with, but it is a lovely face. I've learned to live with it quite nicely."

"Dr. Arnold Dalton," Reggie stated. "You're the one he married? I've worked with Arnold on several occasions when one of my clients got shot up or something. Wonderful guy. I always wondered what lucky woman won his heart. Now that I've met you, I see he was actually the lucky one."

Vivian smiled. "If I'm accurately reading between the lines, you're in love with a pretty special fellow yourself, Regina."

Reggie looked at Derrick, whose eyes were bulging, but she didn't say one word to deny what Vivian had hinted. "Vivian, Vivian, Vivian," he stated. "This is unbelievable. You look incredible, and the way you handled yourself in front of the judge was terrific. I'm so glad things have worked out for you."

"Things have worked out beautifully for me, just as I know they will for the two of you," Vivian answered, speaking to Derrick and Corbin. "As for you, Corbin, there's something I want you to know. I forgave you a very long time ago. That's one of the things I had going for me when I approached your father about allowing me to represent you."

"I didn't remember Vivian's story," Samuel explained. "I'm sure I knew it at the time, but like so many other things, it's gone now. But when she related it to me and told me how she had forgiven you, I instantly knew I had to do the same. Living the rest of my life resenting you would only bring grief to both of us. That's why I hired her to do what she did." Samuel looked over at Vivian and grinned. "The price was pretty high too. She charged me a buck."

"What?" Corbin gasped. "One dollar? You have to be kidding."

"Some things in life are much too important to put a price on, Corbin," Vivian pointed out softly. "The teachings of that Mormon Church aren't all bad, you know. It's my prayer you'll someday learn that for yourself."

Reggie felt the warmth of a smile within her heart as she realized how good she suddenly felt. Today was one of those days she'd remember for the rest of her life.

CHAPTER 25

Bishop Beatty faced the congregation with moistened eyes. Reggie's heart ached for him, as she knew how hard this moment was, even though he would only be saying a few words before turning the time over to her to present the eulogy. She only hoped she could do Samuel Beatty justice with her words.

Clearing his throat, the bishop spoke. "What can I say about my father that those of you here don't already know? He and my mother married when he was twenty and she was eighteen. They had thirty-one wonderful years together. The doctors told Mom she could never have children, but as you can see, she proved them wrong. My brother and I came along ten years into the marriage."

The bishop sipped some water from a glass someone had prepared for him. "Some of you knew my dad as a gold miner," he continued. "Some of you knew him as a free-spirited pilot with a delightful old yellow biplane. Some of you remember him as the creator and owner of a resort where dreams become reality inside its walls. I remember him as my dad and the greatest man I've ever known. As you know, he spent his last years not fully remembering who he was. But this giant of a man didn't let that stand in the way of living every day as if it was the most important of his life."

Lowering his eyes, he paused, obviously too filled with emotion to speak. Long seconds passed. He wet his lips and drew a deep breath. When he spoke again, it was with labored difficulty. "Many of you here have been touched by the generosity of Samuel's heart and the depth of his understanding. When there was a need, my dad was always the first one in line to fill that need. And I want you to know his charity started at home. No one is more indebted to Samuel Beatty than this bishop. And I want the whole world to know it."

Reggie pressed a tissue to her eye as she, too, remembered this great man she was about to pay tribute to. Her mind slipped back to the time he first recovered his memory after having completely lost it for more than five years. Reggie was glad she had been a part of Samuel's return to himself, as well as privy to the heartwarming reunion between father and son. The first thing Samuel did was move back in his old house with Derrick to wait for the upcoming trial of his other son and proceed with living his rediscovered life. Every night, he would pore over the pages of his journals, reconstructing a past the mine explosion had deprived him of.

Even after all these years, thoughts of one particular event brought laughter to Reggie's heart. It had happened the very first time Samuel stepped inside the house. He suddenly wanted to know where his old brown rocker had vanished to. Poor Derrick had tried to argue that the old rocker was nothing but junk and it left him embarrassed when guests came in. "Junk?" was Samuel's own response. "I'll have you know I bought that chair before you were even born, Derrick Beatty. That chair was part of me! How dare you call it junk?"

Reggie had been glad to learn Derrick hadn't disposed of the chair at all, but had only stored it away in the garage under a tarp he felt was worth ten times what the chair was. The chair was immediately restored to its proper place in the living room. Upon first seeing it, Reggie had to agree with Derrick's evaluation that it was an eyesore. But if Samuel wanted it in the house, then that's where it belonged. It remained there until the day the house was sold, and then it became part of the penthouse suite where Samuel spent the remainder of his days running the resort.

A more touching experience came when Samuel related to them the story behind the painting that hung over the fireplace in the house on the island. "It's a terrible thing, not having a past other than what someone else tells you about," Samuel explained. "I think I might have gone mad if it hadn't been for Evelana coming to me." Samuel went on to explain that Evelana often appeared in his dreams, and even though he didn't realize who she was, he painted her portrait from the face in those dreams. "I had no idea why Corbin was so upset the first time he saw the painting," Samuel had explained. "I guess it makes sense in light of what I know now, eh?"

With memories flowing so easily in Reggie's mind, it was only natural that one of a more personal nature should surface. In this memory, Reggie could almost hear the screeching of tires against the hard surface of the landing strip as the little plane set down. She had no idea Derrick had planned a trip to the old mine until his call had awakened her at eight in the morning. It sure beat the first option she had laid out for her Saturday—apartment cleaning.

* * *

Reggie closed her eyes and drank in the tantalizing aroma of pines as Derrick taxied his father's little biplane to the end of the landing strip and cut the engine. Removing her headphones, she turned to see him just climbing out of the rear cockpit. "How was that for a perfect landing?" he asked, moving forward on the wing until he was next to her cockpit.

"As your dad once said," Reggie joked. "'Any landing you can walk away from is a good one.'"

Derrick rolled his eyes. "Very funny, Miss Mandel. So what would you say to a walk in the woods?"

"The woods? Oh, darn, I was kind of hoping for another tour of the mine."

"Yeah, I'll bet," he laughed.

"I didn't bring any granola bars this time," she said.

"Check the side pocket on your seat," Derrick grinned.

Reggie slid her hand in the pocket and removed a package containing six granola bars. "Blueberry-banana?" she teased. "Where'd you come up with that flavor? What's the matter with peanut butter-chocolate?"

"Everyone's tasted peanut butter–chocolate, Regg. Try something new! Live a little!"

"Try something new? This coming from a man who wears the same pair of shoes until they've worn holes in the soles?" This exchange left them both laughing, and Reggie instantly realized there was something different about Derrick that morning. "I can't remember ever seeing you in such a good mood," she remarked. "What's come over you?"

Derrick shrugged. "What's the big deal? I just feel good today!" Reggie knew Derrick well enough to know something was at the bottom of his festive mood, but she couldn't figure what. Glancing down at the disgusting blueberry-banana granola bars in her hand, she tossed them back on the seat. "I think I'll skip the picnic this time around and just settle for the walk. Either give me a hand down or get out of the way so I can do it myself."

Derrick helped her out of the cockpit. They stepped off the wing together and started toward the woods. Reggie glanced down at his hand still holding hers. Not that she objected, but this was a little unusual for Derrick. "What inspired a trip to the mountains?" she asked.

"Like I said, it's a nice day for a walk. Do I need more reason than that?"

She considered this. Derrick could have flown up here with his father or even alone for that matter. Why had he asked her along? After all, they did see each other every day at work. Why, out of the blue, would Derrick want to spend a Saturday with her? And why was he in such a great mood? Then she thought of something she hadn't before. Was it possible this had to do with him running into Vivian Dalton at Corbin's hearing? Reggie had long suspected something in Derrick's past had turned him gun-shy when it came to allowing a woman—any woman—to get close to him. When Reggie had pried the story of Vivian out of Derrick, she quickly reasoned this was the root of his problem. Was it possible, now that he realized everything had worked out so perfectly for Vivian, that he had evaluated some of his own feelings? Reggie glanced again at Derrick's hand still holding hers and concluded this theory must have had some validity. Something had obviously happened to lighten him up. Whatever it was, Reggie liked it, and she intended to make the most of what promised to be a wonderful morning.

Drawing a deep breath, she listened as a few of nature's sounds came to her ears. There was the bubbling of the stream just ahead, the rustling of wind through overhead branches, the song of a bluebird, and just ahead, a few pinecones dropped to the soft earth. How could any morning possibly be any finer?

"The last time we were on this mountain, you tried to push me in the stream," Derrick reminded her. "Just a warning—I'll be watching you this time."

She smiled, remembering. That was the time he almost kissed her. He might have kissed her, too, if he hadn't thought she and Walden Stewart were still seeing each other. Reggie had done some idiotic things in her life, but none more idiotic than thinking she could use Walden to make Derrick jealous. "If I'd really wanted you in the stream that day, you'd have been in the stream," she told him. "I'm just too nice a girl to do that to a defenseless male like you."

Derrick reached down with his free hand and broke off a long-stemmed blade of grass, which he chewed the tip of. After a few moments, he asked, "So, did you miss me the years I was away on the islands?"

The question caught her off guard. Reggie concluded that the mood he was in was really strange if he was asking such personal questions. "I don't know. I haven't really thought about it," she lied. "Maybe."

What he said next came as an even greater shock. "I missed you, you know."

"You did?"

"Yeah. Someday we'll have to go back there together."

"We will?"

"There's so much to take in, so much to enjoy. I'm telling you, Regg, you've never seen an ocean so blue! And the rain forests will amaze you. I could even teach you to surf."

"Surf?" she gasped. "You?"

"Is that so hard to believe?" he laughed. "Just for your information, I'm pretty good at it."

Reggie stopped in her tracks and just looked at him. There was no way she could picture Derrick on a surfboard. "You're kidding me, right? You don't really surf!"

Derrick gripped her hand tighter and led her toward the stream. Reggie wanted to pinch herself to see if this was real or just another one of her nightly dreams about a Derrick who might do something like this. Did he really mean what he said about the two of them going to Hawaii, or was he just talking to the wind?

"You really couldn't have, you know," he stated as they walked.

"I couldn't have what?"

"Pushed me in the stream. If you'd really tried, you'd have ended up pretty darn wet."

"You think so, huh?"

"I know so. I mean, you're good enough you could push most guys in a stream, but not Derrick Beatty."

"That sounds like a challenge," she smirked. "Any time someone tells me I can't do something . . ."

Derrick tossed the stem of grass aside. "Well, here's the stream," he said, just reaching its banks. "Feel free to take your best shot."

Reggie glanced at the stream, then back at Derrick. Was he actually taunting her into trying it? The challenge was just too much for her to pass up. She knew she could never overpower him, but if she could get some momentum going, then hit him just right . . . "Oh, look," she said, glancing off to her left. "It's a patch of wildflowers." Hurriedly, she took the four steps to where the flowers were growing and picked the largest one, which she held up to her nose. "This smells beautiful," she said, hoping to make him think she had forgotten about the challenge. It appeared to be working, as he smiled, then turned to face the stream with his back toward her.

She quickly sized up the situation. He was only about a foot from the water's edge, and he appeared to be concentrating on a little green frog on the opposite bank. She was just far enough away to gain some good momentum with a fast dash toward him. If she hit him just right, she was sure she could force at least one of his feet in the water—which would be enough to make her point. She lunged forward, and as she did, the whole world seemed to move in slow motion. It was too late to back off once she spotted Derrick turning to face her with a most devious grin on his face. Realizing he had set her up, she determined even more to make it happen. She hit him with everything she had, only to end up whirling through the air in the grip of his powerful arms. He spun her in a full circle, then plopped her down on the soft grass, where she lay staring up into those incredible eyes, just as she had stared into them once before— and on this very spot. "You tricked me," she half whispered.

"Like I said, Regg. You're good enough to push most guys in a stream, but not Derrick Beatty."

Derrick leaned forward until his face was only inches from hers. "What are you doing?" she gasped.

Very slowly, Derrick moved two fingers over her lips to silence her. She felt her heart quicken as she closed her eyes and held her breath. *He is going to kiss me!* she told herself. *Please let him kiss me.* Then it happened. After nearly half a lifetime of dreams, the moment came. Very gently, his lips brushed against hers, and it was suddenly springtime. The aroma of pines grew keener, the bluebird's song carried sweeter on the air, and the whisper of wind through the overhead branches swelled into a symphony. As though propelled by some invisible force, her arms encircled his neck, pulling him to her. She didn't even care that her gushing tears were flooding his cheeks. After what seemed like a hundred heartbeats, their lips broke. "You kissed me," she whispered.

"Yeah," he whispered back. "And you didn't stop me."

"No, I didn't."

"Does that mean you liked it?"

Her eyes shot open. Did she like it? What kind of question was that? After all these years, he had finally kissed her! "What do you think?" she choked out, tears of happiness still washing her cheeks.

His only answer came from the depth of his smile as he sat up and pulled something from his pocket. She, too, rose and sat facing him. "The last time we were here I told you something special about this place, Regg. Do you remember?"

Could this really be happening? Of course she remembered. How could she ever forget? But she couldn't give him the pleasure of knowing she had it figured out. Again, she lied. "No, I don't remember you telling me anything."

She instantly realized her mistake as Derrick's eyes lowered in obvious disappointment. "Maybe this wasn't such a good idea after all," he said. "I just sort of thought . . . maybe . . ."

"You said if you ever proposed to a woman, it would be right here on this very spot!" she instantly cried out. To her relief, his smile returned.

"That's what I said. And if I remember right, you thought it was a lame idea."

"Darn you, Derrick Beatty!" she sniffed. "If you're going to propose to me, then just do it!"

Derrick glanced down at the object his hand. "Remember the nugget I found at the back of the mine? I, uh, had it made into this." He held up the most gorgeous ring she'd ever seen. She couldn't take her eyes off it. Of all things—he had had it made from the nugget he found in the mine. It was the most romantic thing she had ever heard. "Did you have two made at the same time?" she asked, instantly wishing she hadn't. What a stupid thing to ask. Of course he would have had a second ring made if he went to all the trouble with the first.

"There may be another one, yeah," he admitted. "But not for your eyes to see yet. The question now is, can I put this one on your finger?"

"You are proposing to me, aren't you?" she choked. "Are you going to get on your knees like you said you would?"

Derrick's grin widened as he slid to his knee. "You had better not turn me down after all this."

"Get to the point, Derrick Beatty! I want to hear the words!"

He cleared his throat and spoke the words she never thought she'd hear from his lips. "I love you, Regg. Will you marry me?"

The second kiss was even more exciting than the first. This time, Reggie could have sworn she heard the sound of fireworks exploding in the sky above them. Or maybe it was just the beating of her own heart.

* * *

"We'll now turn the time over to Reggie Beatty, who has graciously volunteered to share her memories of this great man who was my father."

The bishop's voice drew Reggie from her thoughts. As she stood, it was with a thankful heart for the privilege to speak of a man half as wonderful as her father-in-law.

CHAPTER 26

It had been a long day, but now it was nearly over. Reggie adjusted the sheet on little Christina's bed, then leaned over and kissed her. Pulling the door to her daughter's bedroom closed, Reggie moved to the room across the hall to check on Christina's brothers, Kyle and Benjamin. Satisfying herself they were both asleep, she made her way downstairs, looking for Derrick. She noticed the sliding-glass door leading to the patio was open. Stepping to it, she peered out to see Derrick seated on the porch swing. He was lost in deep thought. She couldn't help but notice how handsome he looked with the light of the full moon peeking through a thin layer of scattered clouds. His hair was beginning to show signs of white around the edges, and she wondered if being married to her the past nine years had anything to do with it. Regardless of its cause, it only added to his handsomeness. After several seconds of just looking at him, she walked to the swing and sat down. He glanced over at her and smiled. "The kids asleep?" he asked.

"Yes, they're asleep. Today wasn't easy for them. They're going to miss their grandfather."

Derrick slid an arm around Reggie. "At least they got the chance to know their grandfather. Things could have worked out differently if we hadn't turned over that final rock after nearly everyone had given up hope that he was even alive."

Reggie snuggled a little closer to Derrick. "I'm amazed at your dad," she mused. "He was wise in so many ways. Wiser than most men I've ever known—even when living the last years of his life unable to remember so many things."

Derrick sighed. "You did a fantastic job on his eulogy today, sweetheart. I know he and Mom were there listening."

"I'm sure they were," she agreed. "But I would imagine they were mostly interested in listening to someone else besides me."

"You're thinking about Corbin, aren't you?" Derrick guessed.

She laughed softly. "Am I always that transparent to you?"

"Just a lucky guess," Derrick chuckled. "I was thinking about Corbin too. He's come a long way in the last nine years."

"Thanks to your father's wisdom."

"That about says it all, Regg. Dad saw something in Corbin the rest of us couldn't. If he'd allowed Corbin to do prison time like we all figured would happen, things would never have turned out like they have."

Reggie had to admit that she had been just as blind to this as all the rest had. But thanks to Samuel's greater wisdom, Corbin wasn't sent to prison. As a result, Corbin learned some critical lessons that changed the course of his life. He learned the meaning of the prophet's words in Alma 41:10, and in the course, he found again a pearl of great price that he had somehow lost along the way.

"My brother, the prodigal son," Derrick commented. "Corbin always wanted to build a monument to our mother, you know. I think he's finally done it. No monument of stone could pay greater tribute to her than the monument of his own transformed life. I like having my brother back, Regg. I missed him all through those years we held each other at arm's length."

Reggie grinned. "Corbin's an all right brother-in-law now, but he was a jerk the first time I met him. He must've known I was a member of the Church, yet he still offered me a glass of wine."

"I'd forgotten about that," Derrick laughed.

Reggie rose and walked to the edge of the patio, where she stood looking up at the dazzling night sky. She felt Derrick ease up next to her. "It's beautiful, isn't it?" he observed.

She laid her head on his shoulder. "Very beautiful," she mused aloud. "And do you know what it makes me think of?"

"No, what?"

"It makes me think of your father. I imagine him out there somewhere enjoying this beauty with your mother at his side, exactly where she'll be from here through eternity."

"Yeah, and you know what else I imagine?" Derrick added. "I imagine Mom telling Dad what a great job her son did conducting the funeral today."

Reggie laughed softly. "What's funny?" Derrick asked.

"I was just comparing the Corbin back then to the Corbin now," she explained. "Then he offered me wine, now he offers the ladies in his life baby formula. I think he looks so cute taking care of our little twin nieces."

"Does it ever feel funny having a brother-in-law for your bishop?" Derrick asked.

"No, why should it?"

"I don't know. Sometimes it feels funny to me, having my own brother for a bishop." Without giving Reggie the chance to respond, Derrick pulled her around to face him. "Have I told you lately that I love you?" he whispered. Again, not giving her time to answer, he kissed her. And the night suddenly became more beautiful than ever.

ABOUT THE AUTHOR

Since grade school, Dan's been busy putting words on paper in one capacity or another. It's been the love of his life. His first novel, *Angels Don't Knock,* was published in 1994. *Lack of Evidence* is his tenth novel, and he hopes to keep writing for many years to come.

Dan lives in Phoenix with his wife, Shelby. They have six children and twenty-one grandchildren whose names all appear somewhere within the pages of his novels. Dan has served in many capacities in the Church and has been a bishop twice and a high counselor four times. He now teaches the fourteen- and fifteen-year-olds in Sunday School, and he says this calling is one of the most fulfilling and challenging he's ever had.

Dan also filled one term on the Riverside County School Board in California and has been involved in other community services as well. Dan loves hearing from his readers, and they can reach him by e-mailing info@covenant-lds.com.